"Not a shade of grey within a [...] The Tryst an unexploded v[...] brightness of Roffey's writing on sex, even as it uncovers inner glades between flesh and fantasy where sex resides - but the taunting clarity of why those glades stay covered. A throbbing homewrecker of a tale, too late to call Fifty Shades of Red."

DBC Pierre, author of *Vernon God Little*

"*The Tryst* is a sly, feral, witty, offbeat erotic novella that unsettles the reader, even as it arouses. There are sex scenes of breath-taking audacity. What would any of us do if an irresistible sex daemon broke and entered our domestic lives, leaving havoc in her amoral wake? Monique Roffey knows that the real question about human desire is whether we even recognise our deepest yearnings. How can anyone resist what they have never even dreamt of?"

Rowan Pelling, editor, *The Amorist*

"I've read *The Tryst* and was enormously entertained and impressed. It's wild and witching, at once contemporary and atavistic, with an anarchic sexual energy running through it and a startling frankness, not only about sex, but about love and relationships, gender and power. . . . a daring write and a consuming read."

Bidisha, writer and broadcaster

"While *The Tryst* offers magic and sensuality aplenty, it lays bare the violence that heteronormative couples will do to 'others' to keep the home system stoked. It can be read as a fable about intimacy and erotic power. Disturbingly, it can also be read as a fable about the socially established vs. the disposable."

Vahni Capildeo, poet, Forward Prize winner, 2016

"A Midsummer's Night Dream meets erotic thriller in this captivating romp through the senses. I found myself laughing, crying and getting beautifully hard as Jane, Bill and Lilah's stories twist and turn through the night and beyond. Monique Roffey perfectly captures the inner worlds of both the unfucked housewife and the archetypal slut in this wonderful tale exploring the power of sexuality, erotic magnetism and the changing face of human relationships."

Seani Love, Sex Worker of the Year, 2015

"*The Tryst* summons your inner whore and demands she be honoured"

Empress Stah, cabaret theatre performer

"Monique Roffey's *The Tryst* successfully straddles mythology and erotica to create a journey towards pleasure."

Suzanne Portnoy, author of *The Butcher, The Baker, The Candlestick Maker*

"Sexy, lyrical and unashamed, *The Tryst* is a powerful slice of modern erotica which blends sexual magick with today's hectic world of male-female relationships."

Vina Jackson, author of *Eighty Days Yellow*

"Sexy as hell. A cross between the work of Angela Carter and Anais Nin, *The Tryst* weaves the urban and the modern with dark myth. Roffey is a risk taking and masterful storyteller."

AJ Malloy, author of *The Story of X*

Monique Roffey is an award-winning writer. Her last novel, *House of Ashes*, received widespread praise and was shortlisted for the Costa Fiction Award, 2014. *Archipelago*, winner of the OCM Bocas Award for Caribbean Literature, was published by Simon & Schuster in the UK, Viking in the US, and translated into 5 languages. Her second novel, *The White Woman on the Green Bicycle*, was shortlisted for the Orange Prize and the Encore Award. Read more about her at www.moniqueroffey.com.

First published in 2017
by Dodo Ink, an imprint of
Dodo Publishing Co Ltd
Flat 5, 21 Silverlands, Buxton SK17 6QH
www.dodoink.com

A CIP record for this book
is available from the British Library

Proofreader: Tomoé Hill
Cover design: Rodrigo Corral
Typesetter: Ben Ottridge

ISBN 978-0-9935758-6-0

Printed and bound by TJ International,
Trecerus Industrial Estate, Padstow, PL28 8RW

THE TRYST

MONIQUE ROFFEY

for
Jan Day
and
Kian de la Cour

"Her mouth is tiny like a narrow doorway, a graceful ornament. Her tongue is sharp as a sword, her words soft as oil. Her lips are red as a rose, sweet with the sweetness of the world. She is dressed in crimson, adorned with all the jewels in the world, with 39 pieces of jewellery. Those fools who come to her and drink this wine commit fornication with her. And what does she do then? She leaves the fool alone, sleeping in his bed, while she ascends to the heights."

The Zohar

1.

MIDSUMMER

JANE

She had pointy ears. Or that was how I imagined them when I first saw her; that's what sprang to mind. She was also curiously hairless, no eyelashes, and her eyebrows were pencilled on. No hair on her arms either, I checked, and her skin, as a result, was more like vinyl upholstery. Smooth and pearly, it stretched over plump limbs and the curves of her face. Her eyes were pear-coloured and slanted upwards, her teeth small and white and neat. Her hair was dyed a flamey red and cut into a bob. The combination made her appear boy-girl. Or perhaps even child. Yes, something about her skin was that new, almost newborn. But her most striking feature was her height, or lack of it.

Lilah Hopkins was freakishly short. She glowed as if lit from within, as if burning with lamp oil, or with the same mysterious phosphorescent substance inside a firefly.

We went to meet Sebastian that night. He'd phoned to see if Bill and I might like to meet for a drink. It was a Sunday evening, a Sunday for God's sake. How could anyone say I'd set it *all* up: I didn't. Not this part. It was a Sunday evening, good and honest, and our journey out was on a whim.

"Let's go out," we said to each other when Sebastian rang; it had been a quiet weekend and I was on the brink of suggesting a trip to the pub myself. Sebastian mentioned a bar he knew, somewhere easy for us all to meet, one of those gastro-pubs, very nondescript. Lots of dark woods, tables, ochre walls, a bar with a stainless steel top, a central island. The place was half-empty when we arrived.

Sebastian was already at the bar, eyes roving the room. I sensed he'd been a bit cooped up and was using us as a prop to get out. No matter. We were using him too in a way and Sebastian is good company, doesn't mind being used. Sebastian is a handsome man, dark curly hair, dark eyes, a cigarette permanently crushed into the side of a grin. He wore battered Caterpillar work boots, a checked flannel shirt over jeans.

Sebastian and I were old friends. We met long before I met my husband Bill, long before I went on my travels. We were part of a small and intimate group of friends, each of us ambitious, aspiring writers or poets, actors and artists. Through our twenties and early thirties we talked and smoked and drank and took drugs and rowed and flirted and fancied and fucked and loved and unloved and dumped each other, swapping partners over and over again. Once or twice Sebastian and I ended up in bed. The first time was glorious, a night I'll remember when I'm seventy years old. The second time was so awful, after a long and booze-fuelled night, I was forever cured of my lust for Sebastian. After that, our friendship became less ambiguous but we remained close. He married a jazz singer, but it didn't last long. Sebastian was recently divorced.

The men hugged and slapped each other's backs.

I kissed Sebastian on both cheeks.

"The longest day of the year." Sebastian held up his pint in salutation.

I had forgotten it was the year's high point, the twenty-first of June, the evening of the summer solstice.

"No wonder you wanted to get out," I teased Sebastian.

"Damn right."

Bill put his hand on my shoulder and ordered us some drinks at the bar. He smelled of sandalwood, a dim scent rubbed into the oakiness of his skin: Bill's smell. He stood close to me, almost touching. He was proud to be seen with me, and I with him. We were together then, very much together, our last hours, before things changed for good.

"You two look well," Sebastian even commented.

We nodded. We *were* happy, pretty happy on the surface of things. We had both showered and made an effort with our clothes. Bill wore a favourite pink shirt, me a skinny-rib cotton polo neck with the sleeves cut away; we were both sun-kissed and lightly freckled from being in the garden. We stood together, blissful in our coupledom; we showed it off.

We found a table in a corner. I sat back, not really listening to the men's conversation. I cradled a glass of merlot to my chest and withdrew. I was happy to let the men talk. They got on well enough. I like that relaxed feeling brought on by alcohol, enjoy the way it slows things down. I was content on the banquette. It was my turn to scan the room which had filled a little since we arrived. I didn't see her then, no red-haired woman caught my eye. There were a few other similar groups in the pub that midsummer evening, mixed gatherings of men and women talking and drinking. Nothing struck me as unusual. I sipped and scanned and daydreamed as I'm prone: my downfall.

It was humid in that bar. The skies bulged and had bled water the day before and the sun had raged that afternoon, then the skies were fierce and empty. It was close, very close in that bar and the heat brought about a tender shine on our faces. My daydream quickly became sexual: a man, faceless, followed me downstairs to the bathroom. Without speaking to each other he had me up against a wall, where he pulled up my skirt, his mouth on my neck, his fingers sliding inside me. I sipped my wine. The man slipped himself into the river inside me. My lips were hard against his forehead, his teeth sunk into my shoulder, both of us trying to muffle the mayhem of arousal.

I kept a dim and remote ear to Bill and Sebastian's conversation while this faceless man held me. We fucked slowly and then less slowly and then faster and harder and then we fell crashing into a cubicle. I braced my legs against the walls of the cubicle and he danced inside me. God it was wonderful, a key in a lock, a piece of my puzzle fitted neatly. We embraced and laughed and fucked in that hot, dark space, downstairs, rhythmic and urgent and ridiculous. My pussy swelled at these thoughts. My nipples hardened. I crossed my legs and sighed and moaned a little. Eventually, I noticed the men's pints were low and rose to buy the next round.

*

When I returned, to my surprise, a woman had joined us. She sat next to Sebastian on a stool drawn in from another table. I assumed she'd just walked in, that she was a friend Sebastian had recognised. Immediately, I was aware of the change this woman provoked in the men's behaviour. Both were far more animated, more upright. Sebastian was visibly more alert, but then this is his way when it comes to women; Sebastian is an alpha male, and charming with it. But my husband too was more alive; Bill had even turned a little pink in the cheeks.

I sat down and coughed loudly.

"Oh, yes. Jane, this is Lilah. Lilah, Jane," Sebastian explained, without glancing at me. His eyes were dilated.

"Well, hello there," this small woman drawled. She was compact, somehow perfect in her dimensions, all curves. I was stunned, staring at her too. She was so . . . bright, her hair beauty parlour red and those ears, subtle and yet blatant, worn with considered intent and daring. I wanted to speak about them immediately, ask about them.

"I'm Lilah. Lilah Hopkins. Pleased to make your acquaintance," her speech was somehow quaint and outdated.

Lilah smiled breezily at me, avoiding eye contact. Her body language implied she knew Sebastian well, that they were familiar: already that vixen was working us. Sebastian gets around so I assumed this woman beckoned from another part of his social life. I was more than a bit put out. Now I could no longer dream away the evening as I liked, sit happily while the men conversed. The atmosphere in our little group had altered. Now a conversation was taking place, one Lilah was conducting. The men were enjoying it. Lilah lit them up. I had to join in. That, or be isolated.

My husband and Sebastian. Two men I knew well, men who were important in my life: men who loved me. Both men were allies. Yet somehow, because of this Lilah-With-The-Ears and mesmeric curves, the way she made them behave, all on edge with wonder, Sebastian talking too much, and my husband all awkward and out of himself, this knowledge was perceptibly undermined.

I remained quiet, observing Lilah, who was talking, talking, talking, beaming, laughing, flirting, all at once. I was immobilised. What did she have that I didn't? What had I lost, and when? Or had I ever possessed it? There was a look in her eye, somehow sly and over-willing. She might do anything, do it then and there. She made us all nervous. Maybe I watched her just like the men watched, unsure of her, half-trusting, half-succumbing. Our reserve dissolved in her effervescence: Lilah had us all enthralled.

I noticed her accent was American. Alabama, she informed us, rather too emphatically. She had been telling the men an involved and far too personal story about herself.

"I was adopted, you see." Her pear-green eyes flashed. "Found on the steps of a church in an itsy-bitsy basket, a pink crocheted blanket over it. Found by one of the good sistahs, Sistah Liz'beth, a saintly person. Found first thing on a Sunday morning, just like a dewdrop. No note. No one knew anything about me. Was taken to the orphanage."

Sebastian nodded with great concern, gazing at her cleavage.

"I was adopted by a fine specimen of a Southern woman. My mama's a redhead just like me, that was why she took me. Wanted a baby who would blend with her looks, who could pass as hers. Mama was a beauty, oh yes. But she married a violent man and we soon departed his company, took the pick-up truck and ran for our lives. She married again, but it didn't work out. My mama's a brave and courageous woman. Five husbands. Five ceremonies. Five deadbeats. Goddamn them to *hell*."

Lilah laughed with contempt. She wore a crimson shirt, tied in a knot at the midriff, a stone-washed denim miniskirt which revealed her short curvy legs. Chunky cork-heeled platforms on her feet. Her finger and toenails were painted black and there were silver bangles and bracelets up her arms, a silver stud in her nose. Her voice was soft, slurred, a practiced and ladylike Southern drawl. Somehow, my immediate dislike and mistrust turned to neutral. I began, like the men, to gape at Lilah. She was a harmless intruder, a naïf. Her brash and over-direct Americanness said it all. I thought she was a novelty, a gay addition to our jaded group. My guard slipped: how did she manage that? I sipped my wine and it went to my head and then I was away again, daydreaming myself into another fantasy with another faceless man. Fancy that, under those circumstances. I was pulled away from those critical moments. Alcohol; I like it like my parents had liked it. I'd inherited a love for intoxication, for getting numb. Did Lilah know this about me? That I liked to drink, slip off into the ether?

Lilah Hopkins talked an awful lot. She twisted her short red hair into tufts, revealing bald underarms. Her eyes twinkled and she curled both hands around her rum and coke, holding it like a child. She wriggled on her seat, tugging at her too short skirt. And she glared at the men in such a blatant sexual manner I nudged my husband in jest. But he didn't nudge me back. Lilah was – well – she was astonishing to behold: wild, reckless with her observations, funny. She swore a lot too, said words like 'fucknuts' and 'asshole'. Everything was 'freakin' this' and 'freakin' that', just like a New York cop. It never occurred to me she might be mixing it all up or making it all up. Her acting was faultless. And, as a result, we were all paralysed, nodding at everything she said. Sebastian showed no sign of leaving. And Bill? Bill was speechless. I didn't know how to play things. And Lilah was doing something strange: constructing a little pyramid of peanuts on the table in front of her, a sculpture she added to, as she talked, with some precision.

"The winters are mild where I come from," she drawled. "But I wish it were summer all year round. Boy, does it rain in the late summer months, Goddamn and hell does it pour and the humidity gets unbearable, like hell's kitchen some days. Sit in a tub full of ice cubes, I do sometimes. Then there are the storms, and the tornadoes; they can whip the earth up into the sky. I come from a place of extreme weather. Twisters, hurricanes. How's your winter here? I'm *dreading* it, I must say. Gonna buy myself a rabbit fur coat, all snug, hole up in it. Gonna buy mitts and a long sheep's wool scarf."

Lilah giggled and her whole body squirmed, as though live fish were jumping under her clothes. There was fluidity in the way Lilah moved and spoke. Like she had a talent for the spoken word; she enunciated her words as though reciting lines.

I sipped and watched and listened to her anecdotes about Alabama. I was in no mood to compete. Lilah looked younger than me by at least ten years. There was something in her eyes which warned me off, something steely-soft, a curl on her lips; also, the rise of her breasts, the way she held them so upright, something about it all said *you're out of your depth*. I didn't gauge her then, her ferocity or potential. Even though she began to make my stomach swim, my veins heat, I didn't assess her accurately. But then, who could? Lilah was something entirely new.

The change she provoked in my husband fascinated me. Bill was devoted to me, had been devoted since we met. It was love at first sight for him. He had never, ever, openly admired another woman in all our time together. But he was gazing, wide-eyed, at Lilah. My dear husband: my other kidney, my sound, reliable, decent, wholesome, utterly faithful husband was checking Lilah out.

She laughed with abandon and again she was a child poured into a womanly outfit. Her knotted shirt exposed her ample breasts. Her miniskirt showed off her rounded hips. This tiny Lilah woman was so damned unselfconscious, that was it. Lilah was bold, unbounded. I even began to like her. I uttered her name under my breath, *lilahhopkins*; I'd never met a person from the southern states of the USA. She seemed incredible, and yet also cheap, like a novelty bar of soap.

Her teeth, though. They were small and neat, yes. Like her ears, they were a little pointy. Oh what manner of creature was she? I didn't see her fully that night in that nondescript bar, barely guessed.

"Gonna buy me some sheepskin boots, too." Lilah winked at Bill.

I watched Bill for his reaction.

"Gonna snugify myself, just like a bear cub in a cave." She giggled again. I found it hard not to groan but I was somehow on the back foot. She held the men's attention like I never could.

Then – Bill flirted. He got drawn out, a first by all accounts. I watched him incline his head and body towards Lilah, as though trying to make himself more attractive. He smiled broadly at her, in a way he usually only smiled at me; he blushed whenever she made a risqué comment. He laughed when she laughed, in fact he laughed at almost everything she said. I watched as Bill peered, thoughtful, into the amber of his pint. I didn't interfere. God, I could have decided to take Bill away, intervene. I could have wrapped the whole evening up with a yawn. Retreated to Sunday evening, to our comfortable world. Returned to our universe, our home, which hummed of two individuals who lived, slept and shared their existence. Headed back to a place of communion, to The Beach Boys in the afternoons and breakfasts in bed. Instead, I watched my husband flirt and Sebastian make his interest in Lilah obvious. Sebastian used all the force of his infamous charm, his eyes dancing over Lilah and his face glowing with expectation of a conquest. Strangely, he wasn't having much luck. It was Bill who Lilah watched.

Then Sebastian's chest erupted with a bleeping sound; his mobile phone had been tucked in his top pocket all night. He took it out and turned away to speak, walking a little away from us, jamming one finger in his ear.

He looked annoyed to be so interrupted. I should have made signs to leave then, said our goodbyes to Lilah and Sebastian, taken Bill home, gone back and gossiped about her, how weird she was.

Instead, I excused myself and went to the Ladies, leaving Bill and Lilah alone.

*

In the Ladies, I peed. I was woozy and woolly-headed, thinking, as I sat, tights around my ankles, skirt around my knees, about Lilah and Bill. And then, about Bill. A tug of war had struck up in me in recent months. It was a war I didn't want; it was making me lose weight. I couldn't placate myself at all. I had no one else to turn to, discuss it with. A row raged over and over, in my head. It went like this:

Do you love Bill?

Yes.

Really love him?

I adore him.

Is he attractive?

Yes.

Then what's wrong?

I don't know. Nothing's there. The love is pure, like no other I've ever known. Too pure.

Too pure?

Yes. Like a love nuns have for God.

What?

Love like a vocation, like a calling. I love Bill like that. Am I the only one who loves like this?

Go ask your friends.

It makes me sad.

Why?

This love has smothered the sex-instinct, cancelled sex out.

What?

I don't want to fuck Bill.

What?

Yes, I know.

Why not?

I don't know. We have been living a celibate life; have done so for the last two years. Maybe longer.

Really?

Yes.

Is this normal?

I don't know.

He's very appealing.

I know. But not to me, not like that.

Other women would like to fuck him.

I'm sure they would.

Are you sure you feel this way?

Yes.

How could this be?

I don't know. Eros isn't part of our relationship.

Surely it was once?

No.

Never?

No.

Then, what happened?

I don't know.

I was miserable with guilt. It was unusual this love I had for Bill. I'd had an inkling of it when we met but never knew how strong this conflict would become. The more I lived with Bill, the more I loved him. I loved him too much: I loved him unfathomably. But I didn't dream of him, not in the way I dreamt of other men, like the faceless man I had just dreamt up in the bar. I had pondered this conundrum for a long time. No answer came. I was trapped inside a monogamous world, inside my marriage, and inside myself. I lived within multiple cases, just like a Russian doll. By day I battled with myself. By night my dreams were besieged by carnal fantasies. Morning dreams too: I would wake with a man I had maybe noticed the day before on the tube, except in my dream he was fucking me from behind, my hands gripping the iron of our bedhead. Or else he was spreading me across a table, my legs parted, my hands flat on the oak. The man was kissing the back of my neck. Or he was pulling at my hair. In my dreams I never saw his face. He was a shadow man, his cock always erect, his hands always firm. Often I would wake with my fingers reaching towards the wetness between my thighs. I wouldn't turn to Bill; I would pleasure myself later, when he was downstairs, spreading my long legs.

*

I rose and pulled up my tights, zipped back my skirt.

I opened the door.

In the bathroom mirror, I studied myself. I was forty-two years old. I'd enjoyed being 'pretty' in the full bloom of youth. I was pale-skinned. My brown eyes were clear, my dark hair shone: an 'English Rose' I'd been called, many times. My face was changing though, undergoing life's grand metamorphosis. All the signs were there: age spots, newly settling crow's feet, grey wisps of hair. My neck was beginning to lose its smoothness. I stared, wanting to step aside, leave behind the image I saw there. I thought of Lilah and Bill, how they were so alive to each other. There and then it came to me: Lilah was the solution.

I left the bathroom and walked back to where Bill and Lilah were engrossed in conversation. I fancied I walked with stealth, as though it was me who had turned predator. I imagined I was sauntering, but in fact I may have stumbled a little from too much wine. Yes, like both my parents, alcohol was part of my downfall. Sebastian had left abruptly, having to meet whoever had called, a drug dealer if I knew Sebastian. It was closing time; the bar had thinned and had that atmosphere of everyone having to leave. I looked at my watch.

"Gosh, it's late," I murmured. "They're going to throw us out. Pity. It's the longest night of the year."

I draped my arms around Bill's shoulders, used my intimacy with him. I smiled and sat down next to my husband, lowering my head across the table, looking deep into those green slanted eyes. What on earth was I thinking? I still don't know. *Oh God, oh God.* I smiled at Lilah as I said: "The night is still young. Why don't you come back to our place?"

LILAH

Bored. I could see she was bored the moment I entered the bar. Withdrawn, watching but not seeing much. Bored and unfucked. I could tell that every time, could see it in every fibre: the way the flesh was dead and the eyes were unglowing and the face looked a little doomed. I could read the prig like a book. Always could. The unfucked always watch, looking out for someone else, for they know they've made a fundamental error. *Wrong, wrong, wrong. I have chosen wrong.* I used to see married human females like this all the time, who'd chosen a man who loved them, who was right in all the other ways, a man who didn't rock the boat, which was why the relationship floated, worked.

The English never knew what to make of me, my forwardness, my daring ways. It was like taking candy from babies. It was always so easy to get laid. I took what I needed from whom I wanted. Easy. But mostly from those couples like Jane and Bill, who had nothing going on down below, no desire between them. It's not a crime or a sin, to fuck a man till he faints, to release some dumb stupid bitch from her own constraints. They never saw me coming, couples like Jane and Bill; they never believe predators like me exist even though plenty of tales of me, and my like, can be found in the ancient books. Modern humans have forgotten them, the impure woman, the insubordinate. I'm the one who ran away. I am there, in their history, those books the moderns no longer read. I often went to bars alone, hunted alone. The English are such hypocrites. Fuck them and fuck their tight-ass Queen.

I saw Bill and Bill saw me. Immediately. He already had the memory of me, all men do. But she didn't notice him noticing me. Didn't see him glance at me several times over by the bar, didn't hear him cough, blush, try to cover himself. Amazing how much a so-called second wife can miss. When the wife-pussy isn't happy, there's nothing to safeguard, nothing to lose. I could never infiltrate a fuck-happy couple. But so few of these exist.

She thought it was all *her* idea! That she set up the entire thing, that it was all her doing. Silly little prig. She had been a looker once and some of that was still there. I could see she once turned heads. Great tits. Nice ass. Good legs. She had a kind of grace she did, Miss Repressed, a kind of – ha ha, impenetrable-ness, little Miss Unfucked, an unused sexiness in her polo neck, her hair tied back. But she was beginning to lose what she'd had and never used, beginning to regret this, I could tell, beginning to fantasise she could have it all back, do it all again. I had it over older women: my pearly taut skin, my edible flesh, my curves and humpable bumps. I had all this forever and ever amen. God I turned myself on looking in the mirror!

I liked the look of Bill, a big-boned voluptuous tree of a man, a mature and bearded oak. All generous with himself, I could tell by his loose and supple boughs, the curve of his stomach, the girth of his thighs, his broad arms. His skin was sun-browned, the colour of heartwood. Our eyes clashed in that bar and he was ashamed and then he was uncertain and tried to look away. But I was taken and determined and knew I'd snare him with all my tricks. Another man sat with them, a different type who saw me too, a fellow predator who appraised me quickly and knowingly. He leered. I smirked with disdain.

I watched and waited.

Yes, Bill. *We've met. I'm the First. I exist in the loins of all men, including yours.*

When Little Miss Polo Neck got up to go to the bar I didn't have to make a move. Both men looked over and smiled at me. Different smiles. Bill's was tentative, a despite-himself smile, curious, intense, unsure of himself. The other man gave me a well-known-to-me, broad and welcoming grin. 'Hello, there, Miss Lady Pussy.'

This with an open-armed gesture.

I slid off my barstool and appeared before them, all radiant four foot ten inches of me. Both men were shocked, impressed. My shortness never fails to make men want to fuck me. My girl-womanliness is a fateful mixture. A fantasy. A child with a whore's smile. The girl-next-door with a cleavage of rare and captivating beauty. Both men gazed at me. I smiled and sat down on the stool the dark-haired man drew up for me. I wriggled, thrusting my tits upward, twiddling my hair. Bill was uncomfortable, I could tell. He squirmed. I loved it all, loved the attention, wanted to take them *both* to bed, take off my clothes there and then. I opened my legs, just a crack, spreading my scent.

"Greetings, my friends. This is a kind invitation."

"I'm Sebastian." The dark-haired man glowed. "This is Bill."

"Am I at Elysian Fields?"

"What?"

Blanche DuBois, of course, a tragic Southern belle of American literature, so pathetic, always made me laugh. I would make these men nervous.

"Oh nothing, just a little joke with myself." I batted my eyelids. The man called Sebastian openly ogled my chest; the alpha human males are so easy to capture.

"I mean I feel fortunate," I gushed. "To make your acquaintance, I'm always so happy to receive the kindness of strangers."

The men stared. My cunt scent had already intoxicated them.

Miss Unfucked reappeared with pints of beer for the men and looked quite rightly startled to see me in their midst. No one explained me properly; I intimated that I knew the dark-haired man. Funny how the English cannot be plain speaking, ask questions. Fishy, awkward, difficult things can happen but they pass by undiscussed; the English are too polite or perhaps too innocent to think the worst. I always took advantage of this to operate. The dumb stupid Queen-ass-kissing prudes. Miss Polo Neck coughed and the men bucked up and I introduced myself, a name I give sometimes: Lilah, I said. Of course, I lay claim to many others. Lilah Hopkins from the Deep South.

I was in control of them then, spinning some crazy outlandish story they gulped down, talking my best deep slurred Southern drawl. Our language has a similar cadence, butter-soft, and we like to use rich sexual words and curse like heathens, so I can easily pass this particular identity off. I told my favourite off-the-peg story, that I was adopted, had been found in a basket on the steps of a church, that my adopted mother had been married five times, that I was a Baptist. They nodded and found this story interesting. Holy God on earth! If I'd told them the Goddamn truth they would have swallowed that whole too, all po-faced and serious, nodding thoughtfully. I could have told them who I really was then and there; they were so nice, so courteous.

Imagine it:

Miss Polo Neck, I have climbed out from between your legs.

I am crafted from impure sediment.

I am the thing that is bothering you.

I have many names.

Storm

Whirlwind

Strega

Screech owl

Child-killer

Strangler

Shedim

Queen of Windows

Thrower of Orgies

Imp

I am your pest, your very own, come forth from all your anxieties, your half-slept nights. From your dream trysts, from where you'd like to be. Oh, yes, I know about them, how you like to indulge yourself, press your hand between your legs and rub. I am from the dark recess of your other life, the life of your unspent lust. I know a thing or two about restlessness. Oh, yes. I am the one who fled. I left my own marriage bed. You don't live as you wish to. You do not love your husband in the way he wants to be loved.

I am your very own thorn.

I am your itch.

Open your legs wider, Miss Unfulfilled.

Instead, I wriggled on my chair and flashed my smooth underarms, and flashed a hint of cunt. I kept up my stories about Alabama.

But Miss Holy Tits fell back, removed herself from the conversation; wisely, she didn't try to compete. She sipped her wine and watched and listened, and I began to grow suspicious. Only she, as women do, noticed my ears, studied them with interest, as she should have, for they are remarkable in the human realm. I never tried to hide my ears. She noticed the charm I was sculpting too, with the peanuts. I know she also found me sexy, all do. I am a spectacle, a work of art, a creature most humans never see in their lifetime. Some half-guess but never trust their intuition, what they plainly see, which is why I often showed off my attributes, my pretty pointy ears. No one ever thought me real or true and so I got away with it. Miss Charity Fuck sipped and stared and guessed half-right, but in the end I don't read minds and was truly surprised by what she did next.

Bill flirted with me and she freakin' watched. She didn't put up a fight, despite her unhappy pussy, didn't snatch him up possessively, which can happen, suggest they go home, take him away from me; she didn't condescend to me outright. No, to my utter amusement, the little prig was also playing a game. And then Sebastian's mobile phone erupted, a relief. He was slobbering over me. He walked away to take the call and then Miss Polo Neck did what no woman had ever done before. Giving me a tight, forced smile she excused herself, leaving me alone with her husband.

Lord, oh Lordy-Lord. Did I ever give the husband a fright. What a sensitive type, this tree of a man. I wanted to have him there and then, put my hand on his crotch, hold him secure in my soft, skilled hands and smile while he stiffened up. I wanted to drop to my knees and bury his cock in my mouth. The females of my race have all been schooled from an early age in the art of Eros. My people have consorted with the tantrikas of India, the mystic Sufis of the Middle East, the Daoists of China, the great witches and sexual magicians of Europe, and we have learnt the art of giving pleasure. We have perfected our own sexual magick. Poor Bill. Little Miss Chastity Belt had abandoned him.

To me.

Lightly, I touched my breast.

Bill froze and stared.

He seemed mortified, longing to gaze at me, trying not to. He couldn't stop himself. He couldn't say anything either; he was shocked and stunned and afraid of me. I smiled as I continued to caress myself, pretending nothing unusual was happening, acted all breezy and happy and all the while I unleashed the force of my nature.

The bar faded.

We stood in a cool glade, around us young oaks, tall and black and slender, bluebells and wood anemone and giant yellow butterflies. This was our lavender-hued country, my true place of residence. Common and also impossible for humans to locate. It isn't featured on any man-charted map, a wood some stumble upon or are led to when lost crossing the Moors, the Great Plains and such like. This edge-land exists in every country on earth, some see it, most humans don't or can't. It can be missed in a blink. It can be glimpsed from the window of a speeding train. In this middle-world the air is thick and gentle with the bustle of stag beetles in the undergrowth and the sigh of toads. It is a still, quiet place. Fragile, like any other woodland.

Bill saw me standing in the glade then and he nodded. He was of the wood too, at least a thousand years of woodsman in him, a man who knew about trees and loved them; he had wood pulp packed up under his fingernails, sawdust in his hair, a love and understanding of nature which is rare in humans. We had stood together before; we had been made for each other. And it had been an error.

And yet, I was moved. We gazed at one another intently. And then I leant forward and spoke to him in my language, whispered to him a poem of love, told him what I wanted to do to him.

I want to hold you in my mouth. Caress the soft sweet clitoris in the back of my throat.

Then I leant over a little closer, exposing my creamy curves. I put my face up close to him and kissed him on the lips, kissed him all tender and villainous.

Then Princess Pain-in-the-Neck returned, drunk and weird and sleazy. She had obviously given herself a pep talk in the Ladies, charged herself with a plan – yes. That was it. She was going to use me. She draped herself all over Bill and Bill looked uncomfortable with this and I nodded, suppressing my amusement. Janey-Wife leant towards me, dropping her head, suggestively, looking at me all eye-to-eye, deeply, all maybe there could be some girl-on girl action, if I was lucky, inviting me back to their house. Well done for bravery, no woman had ever invited me back before. Inside I roared with glee; two for the price of one. What fun I would have with these two innocents. I almost laughed. This was a first: an Invitation From a Wife. A virgin-swinger, a prude, a stuck up little polo neck-wearing, know-it-all prude. Good for her, I thought, silly girl, good for her; she was thinking along the right lines. Good for the queenly prig.

I nodded easily. I saw it all, loved it all. I even wanted to help. I could happily lick her unlicked cunt. I might even have them both, though that hadn't been my plan at first. I wondered what she looked like under her skirt, Little Jane of the Unfucked. This poor woman wanted out, wanted to leave this handsome Bill, get lost; she wanted to get away and she wanted to use me. She wanted me to fuck her husband so she could leave him on the grounds of adultery.

BILL

Like a small speck of heat on my face. A flitting, flickering heat, yes, that was it; Jesus. First, one side of my forehead went warm, then my cheek, my jaw. I felt along that side of my face; why had it gone hot? I turned to see a young red-haired woman sitting at the bar, gazing in my direction. Our eyes met and she nodded, as if to say *hello – yes, you're right. It's me heating your blood.* Then she turned her back on me to face the bar again. I touched my cheek: it was still warm. I coughed and looked towards the bar and the red-haired woman glanced at me again. She grinned and flashed a row of sharp pointed teeth. Or so I thought. I caught a glimpse of her then, of something small and grotesque, something dark, hunched over. An acute fear pierced me. I should have left immediately. Instead, I turned my shoulder on her quickly. I took a swig of beer. I tried to focus on what Jane and Sebastian were taking about. But the back of my neck also went hot.

I knew that Lilah creature was in the bar from the moment she walked in. What were Jane and Sebastian talking about? I couldn't say. I contributed in some way, nods, yeses, nos. Sebastian is a garrulous talker and it's easy to be passive in his company, though I think he was distracted too. He kept peering over my shoulder to the bar. Yes, that Lilah creature was pestering us *both.* Jane, thankfully, was oblivious, sipping her glass of wine, all dreamy and detached. Damnation, what was she dreaming about?

I tried to keep up with what Sebastian was saying, something blokeish but funny, something crass but intelligent. Sebastian can make me laugh despite his extreme attitudes. Jane was tolerant around the two of us, sympathetic man company. She liked to listen mostly, though sometimes she could stop us dead with an observation, shred us up. But that night she was quiet and watchful, as usual. I didn't mind that she'd once had something with Sebastian. They were friends, old friends, and there was no 'unfinished business', no games. But all the while I listened to Sebastian I was aware of the heat on the back of my neck. I'd been picked, singled out for her attention. My body was alert to the heat she spread though me, so much so I twisted around in my seat. I turned around again. The red-haired woman grinned with pleasure at my torment. She turned her back on me in a flirtatious manner. I was determined to stay focused on our group. I took a handkerchief from my pocket and wiped my neck. Jane got up to get a round of drinks and I almost wrenched her back down onto the seat. *Stay, stay*, I wanted to shout. I didn't want her to leave us alone, but I couldn't go to the bar for drinks, didn't dare find myself up close to that creature.

"Are you okay?" Sebastian asked, not really concerned. But he had noticed I'd gone hot.

"Of course," I lied.

When Jane left our table – it was incredible. Lilah willed us to turn round. She probably used this power when on the hunt, some way of pulling the reins, jerking men's heads around. Sebastian and I looked across at the red-haired woman. Me with great unease and mistrust, Sebastian with a wide-open smile, gesturing with one arm in an inviting manner. This was all she needed. She slid from her barstool and stood before us – a shock to see how short she was, a freak. Tiny but radiant. Twinkly green eyes and pearly skin, a crimson blouse which was knotted to expose her midriff and cleavage. The pull was immediate, in the groin. I could have thrown myself on her right there. I coughed to hide my embarrassment. I wanted to fuck her, rut with her, run with her, take her into the forest, there and then. My scalp prickled. My skin crawled with premonition.

Lilah looked like a child. Except there was a mature womanly softness in her eyes, a woman's smirk of sexual confidence on her painted red lips. Sebastian drew up a stool from another table and she sat down, introducing herself. "Lilah," she said. "From Alabama." Nothing feral about her then. Up close Lilah was just like a human woman, warm, but in some way even more succulent to behold. Her skin glowed; faint blue veins swam underneath. She was somehow clean, walked out from under a waterfall or river stream. Clean as a tree. Sebastian and I were felled. I couldn't speak.

"I've come such a long way," Lilah batted her eyelids. "To meet such fine examples of men. You just wouldn't believe how far I've come. Such a pleasure, if you don't mind me saying, to meet two real Englishmen, gentlemen I can tell. Oh, I was getting a little lonesome over there at the bar."

I was unable to look directly into that Lilah-creature's eyes. I remembered her teeth; I stared at her mouth, but didn't see those sharp points again. What had I seen before? I tried to see it again, but couldn't; the memory had been wiped. I took pot-shot glances at this Lilah woman who'd joined our group. Why was she here? Who'd invited her? Where was my wife? I was sullen.

My stomach was knotted. I stared down into my pint. I let Sebastian take charge of the situation, feeling deeply disturbed around this childlike flame-haired woman. Why had she come over? It was hot in the bar, a long hot summer's night. The air was heavy and it made my limbs heavy and my thoughts slow but there was more to it than that.

Jane returned from the bar with the drinks. Her arrival didn't, as it should have, alter the situation. Sebastian practically didn't see her hovering above our table, her hands full, and I . . . well, I was paralysed. It was up to Sebastian to introduce Lilah; he'd invited her over after all, I was sure of that. I assumed he would take her home that night. Jane cleared her throat. Sebastian introduced Lilah and when Jane sat down I could see she was amused and intrigued all at once. Jane nudged me.

"Who's she?" she smirked.

"I'm not sure."

"A friend of Sebastian's?"

"Yes."

"Odd looking, isn't she?"

I nodded.

But Jane's queenly manner soon vanished. Usually it was Jane who reigned cool over most social gatherings. Jane was always the main attraction, well, at least the focus of my attention. But all of a sudden Queen Jane went quiet. I was aware of a contest of some sort, between my wife and the red-haired woman. What was going on? I didn't know. I felt sick and queasy and unsure of myself. My dick began to stir, and that woman knew it. She was making this happen. The arousal I felt was very strong, very instant. My dick stiffened up and I tried to hide it – but it was also a wonderful feeling, to be pulled out of myself. I wanted to hold myself in my hands, pleasure myself right there in the Sunday night pub, while others watched. The urge to fuck this Lilah woman seized me; it spread through me and I was flooded with this desire. *Dear God*, all of a sudden I wanted to unzip my cock and fuck Lilah over the table, spread her legs and release myself into her, nothing held back.

My cool, beauteous wife watched her with a mixture of scorn and alarm. We all watched Lilah. We watched her pale breasts peeking from her red blouse.

Lilah began to talk about herself in a brash but enthralling manner. She swore a lot and laughed too loudly and flashed her eyes at me. She crossed and uncrossed her legs, pulling her short skirt this way and that. I wanted to see up her skirt too. Derision in her eyes; she knew I was trying to spy. Her body was so alluring; I began to feel ashamed. I was staring.

I actually became dizzy with gazing at Lilah. There was a strong scent about her too, earth and something fern-like. I listened to what she was saying: something about her family and being adopted, coming from the Deep South. Sebastian drooled over her, wolf-like, but Lilah could have eaten *him* alive. It was almost a competition between them, who would eat who. I wished dearly that Jane would take me home: *take me home Jane, I want to go, even if it is to our cold bed*. I was miserable, my senses were overloaded. Skin, heart, lips smarting. My dick was rock hard. My eyes were half-closed, as though staring at a bright light. But Jane didn't help; she didn't quite recognise this woman, didn't find it odd she'd intruded. Queen Jane sat back and sipped her wine, unaware of my panic.

Then Jane excused herself to go to the Ladies. It's difficult to explain exactly what happened next. I started to shake – I could feel a crisis happening inside me. A fear which wilted me, made me feel faint. I was gazing at Lilah, as though at a lily or some deep-throated voluptuous flower. Her freckles were like specks of pollen. I stared and shook, with a strong feeling of wanting to put my stamen inside her. I saw an immense and serene woodland, midsummer, sunlit ferns like lanterns. Yellows, greens, and many tall slim black trees, trees like many people, a silent stationary crowd. I was gazing at another place, familiar, yet alien. A notion of kinship surged inside me, a feeling of family. Was I looking at a glade I had visited? A place I knew innately? Lilah stood in the middle of this woodland, thigh-high in columbine and wood anemone. She smiled at me, all naked and clean, long grasses rising up to the auburn pelt between her legs. She slid her fingers inside herself and her body squirmed. These images seemed to emerge from nowhere, from a memory? I felt lit up and also calmed. My dick throbbed with grief, with longing. I felt physically weak, intent on staring into this glade, a scene Lilah was letting me see. Then I understood. She was introducing herself, properly.

2.
THE EGGS

JANE

Every birthday, I gave Bill an egg. It hadn't occurred to me that as I was gifting eggs to him, my own were ageing, or whatever they did. Dying? I understood eggs were a symbol. Eggs are the universe's most ancient cell; all life evolves from an egg. Eggs are perfection itself: steely, benign. Self-contained.

The first egg I gave Bill was made of turned beech wood, grainy and patterned and tan. We were married only a few weeks when his birthday came round. I presented it to him when he woke, in bed, and he loved it instantly. I had to visit my sick mother in Devon soon afterwards, leaving Bill alone for ten days. He told me he kept the egg safe in his pocket and slept for most of that time, clutching the egg, kissing it, rolling it around in the depths of his roomy fleece until I returned. He already had a thing about eggs, had collected them for many years, mainly crystalline, pink and patterned and pretty, eggs that were cold to touch, mottled and delicate. He kept them on top of a shelf in his workshop, piled up in a large glass goblet.

Bill is a big man, six-foot-four barefoot. He has a large oval face, perfect square white teeth. His face is pliant and always different. Sometimes he can appear old and unlovely, run-down; other times he is boyish and cute, even handsome, definitely winsome. His smile transforms his face. Bill has something, a quietness, a gentle disarming charisma which draws people to him. His hair, once chestnut, is flecked with grey, as is his beard. His blue eyes are crinkly, alert. Bill is a cabinet maker by trade, gifted with his hands, descending from a long line of craftsmen. His ancestors were all folk who lived off the Weald in Kent.

It was December when we met: frost on the ground. Short days and long dark nights. The Earth, in the north, had tipped away from the sun. We met through my friend Judy. Bill taught woodwork classes one evening a week and Judy was one of his students. Judy had a crush on Bill, I think; she had hoped, quietly, they might become more than friends. One night, Judy invited me along after their class to a pub in Crouch End. Eight students and Bill. I was immediately interested to meet, well, *see* Bill. Bill is the kind of person you first see.

I retreated into my glass of wine, sipping slowly, falling back, not wanting to talk, just watch. Bill was engrossed in a conversation with one of his male students and I assumed he hadn't noticed me much. Bill drew pictures in the air as he talked, the gesture pulling up his shirt enough to expose a once muscular, but now ample stomach. Bill has shape, a figure, mammalian hips which curved outward like a woman's. His legs are long and elegant; his arms are muscular. His movements are slow, yet he has the poise of a ballerina, as though demonstrating how a big man can get about without knocking things over. I filtered the conversations around me out so I could only hear Bill.

"Trees die on their feet, they do," he said. "When they're ready. They dry up. Keel over. A kind of suicide. Noble, really. England's trees are difficult to kill; most can survive felling, ring-barking. And they don't burn too well either, burn like wet asbestos. Can't clear a British forest with fire, oh no. To burn our trees you have to cut them down, chop them up, and then stack the pieces."

Five days after our meeting, Bill rang.

"Is that . . . Jane?" I could sense the pain of modesty in his voice, that he was nervous.

"Yes."

"Judy gave me your number, she mentioned that you work for . . . I mean that you were part of a, well, I . . . er. I was sorry not to speak to you the other night. I thought maybe you might be, I mean, might like to . . ." A pause. He was asking me out. What a welcome surprise. I loved him then. I had already started loving Bill.

"I'd love to."

"Thank you." A sigh escaped his lungs. I heard him checking himself. "I mean, I'd love to too."

"Where?"

Our first date was in an old pub in the East End with a roaring fire in the hearth and a woman singing ballads on an acoustic guitar. My heart quaked as I walked through the door, and, when I spotted him, I planted both feet on the ground, earthing myself. I was scared. Years since I'd been on a date. I had dressed and undressed several times, opting for jeans in the end, boots, a heavy sheepskin coat. Bill was nervous too, even though he appeared comfortable by the fire. Beads of perspiration sprang from his forehead as I sat down.

"Martians?" I said.

"What?"

I pointed to the cover of the book he had with him, open, on the table.

"On the cover. What are you reading?"

"Oh, some pulp fiction. To hide behind. Wasn't really reading it."

He gazed up at me. "You look lovely."

The evening didn't go well. Both of us awkward and yet wanting to be there; no chaperone or mutual friend to ease the silences and to hide or excuse the reason for meeting. All those questions. And answers – and staring at each other, sizing each other up. How did my past sound to him? My parents both alcoholics, many of my friends too, and most of my past lovers. I had travelled, seen the world. Partly to get away from them all. I hadn't wanted to be married. I liked children, but there'd never been a strong urge to have my own. I'd always had a keen sense of needing to get out into the world, fulfil my potential. Bill's calm friendly manner was unnerving. I skimmed the facts of my past as much as I could. Mostly, I wanted to hear about him, wanted nothing of who I was.

What do *you* do?

Where were you born?

Marriage?

Family?

Friends?

Who do you live with?

What state are you in, now you've passed forty?

How have you coped with failure?

These questions lurked, welled in my throat.

Bill, it turned out, was divorced, the father of two. He lived alone with his cat, Choo Choo. He had survived a bout of post-divorce depression. He briefly mentioned his ex-wife and when he did his face darkened. I sensed a great and not-so-distant pain in his heart.

Strangely, the wine didn't go to my head. The more I drank the more sober I became, the more a headache set in. I rely on it so much, to help ease everything; this time it didn't work. We moved on to another pub, where a person he knew appeared and gatecrashed our table, a bore Bill disliked but was too gentlemanly to chase away.

We left at last orders, standing on the pavement outside, both tentative. Light flakes of snow spiralled from the black sky, descending on us like a quiet blessing. I held my palms out flat and open to catch the flakes. Bill placed his hands under mine and we stayed there for several minutes, catching snowflakes. Both of us were unsure with each other. We both wanted to try love again; there was a sense of that between us.

"Goodbye." I smiled. Bill squeezed my hand in his, forming a small, perfectly round snowball.

Our second date went better, a day trip to Kew Gardens, wandering through greenhouses, the grace and splendour of those Victorian glass structures, the narrow walkways forcing us close, the mist on the panes. I was captivated and slowed down. It was like we were on holiday in an experiment. We stood for minutes gazing upwards at the travellers' palms. What continent had they come from? Who had brought them to London and when? Outside we marveled at the frozen lake; we walked in step, it all felt so natural. No tension, no drama; I felt comfortable with Bill, like we'd known each other a long time. Bill exuded a soft manliness, a faded handsomeness. Later we drank mulled wine in the café. Fewer questions: lots of gazing into Bill's open face, watching his movements. We sat without touching, spoke and listened in turn: hours in that café.

Our third date went better than the second, a walk from King's Cross to Camden along the canal, walking past London's community of canal boats, tough living in the winter. But walking along the towpath was again somehow intimate, narrow lanes, people riding past, Bill's protective hand on my back. We stopped and had lunch in a brasserie. Chestnut soup. We dared to hold hands across the white linen tablecloth. Again the subject of his ex-wife came up. I sensed there'd been more trouble than he could cope with. He'd seen a therapist for years, admitted to using Prozac. Both had helped. He said that for many months he hadn't been able to get out of bed. Bills went unopened, debts mounted. CCJs, the bailiffs had come round. A friend had stepped in to help sort out his paperwork. I understood. And I was glad we hadn't met then, when he'd been in the first flush of this grief.

I lay in bed and thought about Bill between each meeting. I enjoyed the slowness of our courtship; even then I was beginning to miss him between each meeting. Christmas approached: the winter solstice. Another year dead: I was thirty-seven.

I tried to imagine sex with Bill but couldn't. I tried to imagine my legs wrapped round his thick trunk, but couldn't conjure up the image. I pleasured myself in the mornings, distracted and out of myself; I was alone and yet somehow in love with Bill. How could this be? I went to visit my mother and some family friends for a week. Bill spent part of Christmas with his sons. When I returned, in the New Year, there was a heart-shaped wreath made of holly and fir cones pinned to my front door. A card though the letterbox.

Bah Humbug.

Christmas was no fun without you.

I had missed Bill too. But I was unsure of myself. I simply took small but forward steps towards Bill. Every meeting was another part of him to think about; Bill was so many things: faded, failed, glamorous, sad, solid. Bill was mature too, and stable. He was a father, which gave him an advantage and meant there was no pressure between us to have children. Bill had been somebody's husband and he had been badly hurt and had risen again, to face the world. Bill was remade. Bill won me with his open face, his easy nature.

But it was Bill's workshop that clinched it. Date four, January. After a day trip to the seaside in Rye, we drove back to his house for tea. The workshop was a garage once, quite large, at the back of his house, the kitchen looking out onto it across a cobbled courtyard. A galvanised tin roof, glass panelled wooden doors. Inside there were benches and trestles on which he worked. Wood chips and sawdust on the ground.

Everything was housed in Bill's workshop: rows of bleached white animal skulls. Femurs and tibias and other bones all arranged like tools. Bicycle parts, handlebars and bike seats, lights, bells, pedals, wicker bike baskets. Footballs too, thirty or so, piled in dustbins in one corner. Lampshades, like an array of wedding hats along one shelf, wooden chairs hung from hooks in the walls so they appeared to be levitating. An old Chesterfield sofa in another corner, an enamel casserole pot as one leg. Parts of cupboards, beds, bedheads and bedknobs in baskets on the floor. Railings, cornice pieces, curtain rods. Wheels, in dozens of types and sizes, all pinned to the wall suggesting a huge machine embedded behind the plaster, a steam engine? Laundry baskets full of pieces of iron. Many objects I couldn't identify. Jars of brushes and screwdrivers and row upon row of hammers and pliers and great bow saws and handsaws and mallets and vices. Leather aprons and gloves, goggles and welding guards. The objects were still, sculptural. Refuse exhibited as art; curated, cared for.

A feeling descended: here was peace. Here, a world. A keen sense that all the love in me could finally be released. My love had found a place of residence. My eyes became wet. Quickly, I wiped them dry.

"Are you okay?" Bill enquired, worried.

"I'm fine. Dust."

There was lots of wood too, in Bill's workshop, baskets full of wood: oak, ash, hornbeam, cherrywood and beech. Planks had been rescued from skips, from demolition sites, also oars and fence posts. Branches too had been collected; and tree stumps and baskets full of brambles shorn of their thorns, all coiled up so they resembled reels of cable.

A memory: Bill sitting on a rickety reclaimed chair, shrouded in furls of blue smoke from his Camel cigarette.

Choo Choo, his great fanged ginger cat, on his lap. As he stroked the animal gently, he talked about the months of depression following his divorce.

"I have my life back again," he said in a careful, wistful tone. "I'm interested in the future."

I sat at the other end of the workshop, perched on what might have once been a pram, sipping tea, quietly, wondering. Bill's house was dilapidated, a hovel. His real abode was his workshop. I'd never met anyone like Bill. On the face of it he was broke, divorced and a father of two. But also Bill was focused, restored anew: his ambitions were for his hands only. All this attracted me.

*

I grew impatient for a kiss. Something was happening between us, but not in the usual manner of things. Bill filled me with a feeling of buoyancy, a compassion of the soul. Our minds and hearts had met, and yet no sparks flew between us. I was perplexed. Was the attraction physical? If not, what kind of attraction was this, what kind of love was growing between us? Why had his wife left? He never fully explained; had there been an affair with another man? Had he been cuckolded? There was something I couldn't put my finger on, even then. Something I buried. I liked so much about Bill. We were taking things slowly and yet we were mere humans, half-blind. There was part of him I couldn't reach.

"When are you going to kiss me," I asked, eventually. We had been courting for weeks. He looked confused, happy and taken aback. He had been biding his time, waiting for the right moment. He bent and took my face in his hands and he kissed me gently on the lips.

It turned out Bill was no shy lover. Nothing slow or awkward or unsure about himself in that way; he'd just been waiting. Bill made love to me – starting with my feet. He kissed each toe, each bone in my ankles, kissed my arches, kissed his way up my shins, behind my knees, working his way upwards, parting my thighs. I gasped, my hand reaching down to stroke his head.

"Pretty, you're so pretty there," he murmured, gazing at my vagina. "Like tiny open petals."

He kissed me there and I squirmed. Bill kissed and kissed and kissed me there, his head sunk, murmuring half-words, lost sentences.

Bill was ready and able to love again. He loved his work, his children and life. He held a belief in God which was personal, natural. Bill was good at love. He loved me from first sight in the pub, it was a love which never wavered and only grew. I walked into Bill's love. It was the opposite of all I'd ever encountered before. Before Bill, there had only been obsessive loves, loves that had burnt and crashed. Men who meant nothing to me once the haze of lust had cleared. I had only been star-struck by fools, false loves. I had loved lesser men. I thought – *I am safe.*

The eggs? They became something more. They became a measure, a unit of time, a tiny monument, a memento of our time together. Privately, I marked us out in eggs, each egg representing a year. 'Eggs were us'. I developed a superstition that each egg was vital, that somehow we would stop being together if the egg gift wasn't given. I imagined our years together as a row of brightly patterned eggs, fancifully thinking of all the different types of eggs I would give Bill: exotic, cheap, funny, pretty, gold, eggs from rare birds. I liked to look ahead and think of the next egg I would give. I began to search a month before his birthday, never knowing what I would find. I began to worry if I didn't come across an egg in the shops – then I would search more intently. I don't know why I became so obsessed. But I did. I thought the year I didn't give Bill an egg something bad would happen.

3.
THE HEX

JANE

There was a moment between us: Lilah's eyes glinted at my suggestion. We both understood what my invitation meant – I was giving over. Bill didn't notice we hadn't exactly hit it off: *they'd* been talking. Lilah and I had barely said a word to each other. I'd been watching only, taking Lilah in. I wasn't abrasive or cold; I had kept my body language neutral. Bill had taken this for friendly. An innocence exists amongst heterosexual men when it comes to women. Bill didn't, for a moment, suspect *I* might want to sleep with Lilah – or that we might all end up in bed.

Bill didn't find it strange I'd invited her back. Didn't protest or make a face, shoot me questioning looks of disapproval. I didn't give him the opportunity, either.

"Come on – let's go then," I commanded, sweeping them up and out of the bar, hailing a cab on the pavement. I might have invited Sebastian back; we sometimes have friends round of a Sunday evening. Bill didn't seem to mind at all; he was meek, resigned to having Lilah along. Bill worked from home and didn't need to get up at any specific time the next morning. And the night? It wasn't even fully dark, yet. The night, that night, the longest of the year, was still young.

Lilah sat between us in the cab on the journey home, her pearly white legs flashing as she rambled to Bill. She talked on and on in her feminine Southern drawl, regaling us with stories of her saintly band of aunts and cousins.

"All women, all Baptists. Bless their souls. I escaped the South, a sinner, oh Lord, forgive me and my sinful ways. But I still love them all. Though they aren't my real family . . . I was adopted," she explained. But it sounded like it was the other way around: like Lilah had adopted *them*, made them her brood, her responsibility. I rooted myself in the corner of the cab's seat to gain some distance, my face flush to Lilah's profile.

I had a good look at her ears. A little too large, and tapered to a point. Natural on her, though. She wore them as another woman might wear a large bosom or beauty mole. Her hair was parted behind and in front so they protruded like two dainty ears of corn. While some women know they have magnificent hair to show off, or a fabulous behind, Lilah had ears. They'd puzzled and attracted Bill. Drawn him in. He found her enchanting and I could see why. Lilah looked as though she had stepped out from off the top of a birthday cake. From out of the Playboy Mansion, all bunny-tailed and pert. Part luscious belle, part something else, baby animal? She was so small and tidy. Americans. I thought – with some condescension – she is American after all, a Southern bumpkin.

Even so, my stomach was tight, churning. My plan, so far, had worked. I had got Bill drunk, propositioned Lilah, captured Lilah and Bill together. We were speeding home. Then what? Then what – I asked myself. More drinks? Lights? A disco in the kitchen? It was hot in the cab and I wound down the window, stuck my head out and let the breeze whisk my hair. Our home was round the next corner, warm, a haven: what was I was bringing with me, a whirlwind, a dust devil? I didn't know, I didn't realise that it was me who was the naïf, the bumpkin.

The cab stopped and we got out. Bill paid the fare and led the way down the front path to the front door, Lilah was in the middle and me behind. No light conversation between us, not one of us spoke; Bill seemed morbidly deep in thought, or drunk, or both. Lilah was like a deer as she high-stepped the lavender and daisies beside the path, they swished her thighs. The top right window of our home shone with light, beckoning us inside.

*

After we were married I moved in with Bill, into a crumbling but spacious Victorian terrace which his mother had left him. The bottom floor was our living space, a large separate sitting room with a dining area and kitchen at the back looking out onto a courtyard garden. Upstairs, two more floors, mostly bedrooms and my study. Our home was book-stuffed and full of treasure we'd found on beaches and river trips. The walls were crammed with paintings; the furniture was mostly crafted by Bill. Before I moved in the walls were nicotine-stained and drab. Together we painted them mustard yellow and tomato red, pistachio green. The wooden floors were bare and we threw down rugs. Bill, Choo Choo and me lived there.

But Lilah didn't notice anything, not a picture, not a book. She drifted through our home in a switched-off manner, gazing around with a blank expression. Homes are exhibition spaces and we all like to snoop.

But Lilah seemed blind, unlooking. Oddly, she paused in the kitchen and looked perturbed at the sight of the cat's bowl on the floor. She reminded me of Choo Choo: silent, graceful, self-contained. And as for Choo Choo, where was he? Usually, he greeted us when we arrived home, weaving himself amongst our legs.

"Choo Choo," I called.

But he didn't appear.

Bill mixed Lilah a rum and coke, poured me and himself malt whiskies. I needed the whisky, wanted to knock the whole lot down in one. Instead, I cradled the glass, withdrew again, sat down opposite Lilah. We had retired to the sitting room and Bill put on some music. Lilah's face lit up. She was enveloped in our large and comfortable sofa, her miniskirt revealing full thigh and curvaceous calves. If we had all been a little drunken earlier, now no one was remotely drunk. In fact, we were all sober with the alcohol, with the heat, with the night which was by no means over. Bill and Lilah were merely mellowed by the last few hours of conversation, by my sanctioning presence. Already it had all gone too far: I was allowing what no woman would. I felt like a swinger. Wasn't this what they did?

Bill's mood had lifted; he seemed casual, almost too casual, and relaxed, referring to me at times, like an old friend, in the third person.

"Jane can't count too well, not great at maths. She once paid . . .."

She this and *she* that. I was disappearing before my eyes. Lilah knew it; she smiled with inner certainty, our collusion was silent and it was working. If Bill and Lilah were in the midst of a first date, it was going remarkably well. They looked good together, physically at ease. This stung me. I had brought her here. I cleared my throat.

Lilah stared.

"What is it, dear?"

Lilah winked at me, half-smiling. *I dare you*, her eyes teased. The game was on. Fuck her, let them fuck each other.

"I'm beginning to wilt," I spoke into my glass and drained the whisky.

Lilah sneered.

I returned her sneer, levelling my gaze. Our eyes locked, briefly. *Go on, then.*

"Darling, I'm going to slip off. Don't stop chatting on my account." I smiled, reassuringly, at Bill. His eyes were concerned, but not too concerned.

"Are you sure?"

"Absolutely. Early start tomorrow. Lots to do."

Lilah nodded politely.

I stood up and kissed Bill on the forehead quickly.

"I'll be up soon," he said.

I peered down at Lilah. Her pointy little teeth. A flash of something dark, hirsute. Hunched over? I flinched. I blinked and looked again. The dark creature vanished. Had I imagined it? Lilah fluttered her eyelids coquettishly at me, sipped her rum and coke. *Just get on with it*, I seethed. I wanted her to do what she had come to do, what I wanted her to do. I was quietly, miserably, unsure but also, somehow, pushed. I didn't say goodbye to Lilah and Bill didn't notice. I nodded, leaving the room, climbing the stairs, where, once in our bedroom, I shrugged all my clothes to the floor and fell into a heavy sleep.

LILAH

We rode back to their place in a London black cab, all three of us in the back seat, and boy did I get creative with the Story of My Life: seven aunts, all saintly, strict churchgoers, me a sinner. How, even though I was adopted, I looked after them and loved them and provided for them but eventually had to escape the responsibility. There I was – freakin' sandwiched right in between Bill and Maid Marion. Rubbing shoulders with both of them, all skin-on-skin, knees touching. Both stared at my curvy legs, down my shirt, Bill became more relaxed, forgetting his fears. Down one side our bodies were sealed together, hips, legs, moulded comfortably. I sensed that already it had begun between us; I hoped that Wifey Poo would quickly leave us to it.

I knew she was having a good look at my ears. I wore them like other women wear earrings, hair parted to show them off. But the little prig didn't know I could hear her heart beating so quickly, *thumpety thump thump*. I could hear her swallowing her saliva in great gulps, hear the perspiration break out under the line of her bra. *Drip, drip, drip*. Yes, that's right, take me home, Snowdrop. Ms Dry Cunt of the Domestic Trap. Take me to your Vanilla Parlour of Comfort and Taste, take me to see your Nest, your Happy Home, yes take me back to your home-sweet-home. I loved it when people stared at my ears, I felt proud of myself. So I kept up my steady babble about the South, about my aunts, about the scholarship I had won to study in London. I talked and talked and smoked a ciggie and crossed my bare legs suggestively and even the cab driver gawped at me into the rear view mirror, wondering who the fuck I was – and what was happening. I winked at him and flashed a little cunt. *Lordy, Lord.* A Sunday night and an atmosphere of Saturday night, late Saturday night, in the back of his cab. The scent of the woodland pervaded their midst, fern and spore of puffball and leaf mulch clamoured for release. I had brought all this with me from deep in the black earth of the woods.

Their nest, as I predicted, didn't interest me much, but I'm sure it was a source of pride to them. Like a little museum, a clean one, showing off their life, their idea of good living. I quite liked the furniture, though, which I could see was all hand-crafted, made by Bill. I could tell she wasn't pleased I didn't poke about, didn't *ooh* or *ahh* at anything. I noticed the eggs, though, three of them, displayed on the ledge of a bookcase, little totems. Her infertility symbols. Each marked a year, I guessed, a year of their marital relations; they marked out her secret – that she was counting. Actually counting out her years, just like prisoners do in gaol, scratching days out on the wall of their cell. Three years of prison. She was a hetaera woman, I was sure. The eggs said it all, the lack of children. She just hadn't figured out her true nature; most modern women don't and now there are droves of these types. Educated and hip, good-looking too, they want to be out in the world. Their type is ancient, a relative of mine, you could even say. There was the proof. Three of her own withered and unused eggs displayed like sacrificial effigies – Holy God on earth.

Then I noticed a cat's bowl on the floor in the kitchen; this threw me. Cats know instantly. I made a mental note, briefly. Bill mixed me a rum and coke and Miss Frigid Face a stiff whisky and we sat round their coffee table and I could see she was nervous and unsure and wanted to know more about me. Her silly plan had worked. She tried to stare me down, but I was already in the door, all comfy on the sofa, ready to fulfil her rotten motive. In her perfect house, she had brought me here to fuck her husband – and I couldn't wait. Move over. Go to bed Wifey, night, night Wifeykins. Bill, bless the fool, was completely innocent of our doings. Had no idea. How could he know? Not a word had been exchanged between me and his lovely Janey-Wife. He was already referring to her without significance, as though she were a friend. *She* this, *she* that, as though she were somewhere else. *Dear* this and *dear* that. Bill hardly batted an eye in her direction, how could he?

I glowed, all young and fresh to look at.

Just like a dewdrop.

A pearlified ray of light.

An ant egg.

A rain spot.

Full as a harvest moon.

I was his first.

I was made for him.

I am the one who refused to lie down beneath him.
Beneath any man.

I am insubordinate.

A pest.

A djinni.

Darkener of the Daylight.

Some nights I simply stand there, in the widow of a house, any house I choose, and whistle to men.

And they come.

How could Janey-Wife compete?

She soon feigned tiredness and stood up and she kissed him on the head, like a mother might kiss her son. All so tricksy and yet so acceptable, leaving the likes of me there, alone with him.

My eyes were as wide and luminous as the moon, my skin plumped up. My nostrils tingled. The small bones in my ears danced, hearing the tension in him, the skin of his temples tightening, the muscles in his neck straining; I heard his deltoids tense, his glutes flinch in anticipation of what was coming. I heard his knee joints cracking, his hip joints floating in their bowl of gelatinous fluid. My nose twitched. I regarded Bill with intent, imagining what part of him I would eat first.

Bill was shaking when I approached him. God, it was a warm night. His face shone with the heat and I found this so enticing. He shook – with guilt, with the shame of his impending infidelity. I advanced anyway, with great care not to spook him. I climbed on to his lap, my knees bent each side of his thighs. I watched his face, his eyes flit from side to side. I watched his hair grow, his pores open, his skin breath. But soon the worried expression on his face softened.

"I won't hurt you," I whispered.

He laughed. But his face was serious and water appeared in his eyes. I laughed too, taking up his fingertips, pressing them to my mouth, beginning my slow and steady process of giving everything – little strumpet that I was – starting oh so slowly with this gentle man. I licked the delicate crotch-web between his fingers, watched him squirm. His eyes fired up. I licked his wrists, the pale skin on the inside of his arm, the kissing point of the inner joint.

Still, he didn't understand who I was, where I'd come from. I kissed him full on the mouth, drinking him in and he groaned with pleasure and a small measure of understanding, surrendering – *ahh* – I sighed with the pleasure of conquest. I promised myself I would be good to this one, I wouldn't be selfish. I liked this Bill, I liked his hands on my thighs, the sorrow in his eyes.

Bill was okay then.

Slowly, I began to unknot my shirt. The buttons I took one by one, from the bottom. This caper I learnt from Miss Garnet Frig, an English stripper, a fat bottle blonde with pendulous breasts and a voluptuous ass. *Start from the bottom, and work your way up*, she advised. The best way to tease. And tease Bill I did, tweaking my blouse open, feeling the hardness of his cock between us. One button, then two, my skin like milk satin underneath. Bill watched like a man, not a boy, openly admiring, hard as wood under his jeans. I gazed deep into his eyes, the biggest tease of all; would he continue to look into my eyes as I revealed all? I pulled my shirt open. My breasts had stiffened to points. I ran my fingertips over them and smiled at Bill all the while. There they were, revealed, two white mountains, tender and slutty and ripe. Each with a tiny, moist, red rosette mound.

Bill kept gazing deep into my eyes. I smiled, then pulled the shirt from my shoulders so that I was naked, from the waist up. I was still astride him. I pressed his palms to my breasts. His instinct for my flesh was immediate, a light caress, in harmony with the way I like to be touched. His touch was tenuous at first, as though feeling his way, all the while looking into my eyes. A touch so light it was a surprise, him being a man who worked with his hands. But his fingertips weren't calloused. My skin rose up.

I gasped.

He smiled and raised his eyebrows as if to say, *good*?

I nodded. I looked down at my breasts.

He followed my gaze.

Usually I'm in control of these moments with mortal men. But Bill turned my face back to him, holding me in his vision, a strong masculine gaze of intent. His cock between us, hard and yet not urgent, or needy. I could have straddled it then, but I didn't. Most men would have been excited, might even have lunged. There I was, luminescent, naked, and he still hadn't lost himself. Then he was caressing me, my collarbone, my throat. He was touching me like I touch myself in the night, when I'm alone and aching to be touched. My breath quickened, my cunt was dripping.

Bill traced his hands, his fingers, ever so lightly downwards, to my breasts, gently caressing the tips of my nipples with the hollow of his palms. I arched backwards and thrust my breasts forward, all glorious, and yet he didn't grab or bury his head. He traced circles and I groaned. Then he pressed one hand flat to my heart, the other between my shoulder blades. He rocked me back and forth, and it was then that I reached down and unzipped him from his jeans. As he caressed my breasts, I caressed his long sturdy cock.

An old Jesuit priest taught me how to touch cock. Oh yes, he did. Father Joseph from a monastery in the valleys of western California; he showed me how men like to be pleasured, all steady and yet fluid, just like women like to be touched. He showed me all manner of grandiose hand job, each with a name, the twisting juicing movements, the double hander shakes, how men love to have their foreskin gently scraped with the back of fingernails. Of course, Father Joseph left the brotherhood eventually and got a job in a swingers' sauna, which is where we met. Father Joseph is famous in certain parts of California. And so I gently scraped at Bill's cock, running my nails up and down the shaft and all the while he lightly kissed my breasts, his beard all grassy, like a great sea sponge. He laughed with a kind of dazed amazement.

Oh – what a pleasant surprise. This Bill was a Lover, after all. Not a Fucker, like the majority of human males. Not all please-my-cock-now neediness. He had skill and timing and he knew how to give, how to meet a woman and see to her needs before his own. This was a first. I was surprised then and made a small mental note. *Be careful.* But I wasn't worried, no – why would I be? In all my adventures on earth, I had finally met a man with some skill. I was pleased, not alarmed.

*

Our people are a race of Lovers. We believe the love act should, ideally, last for hours. We are small, yes, but well-endowed with patience and stamina, a great generosity for the carnal arts. We are a race of sexual connoisseurs who know how to copulate, be it the tenderest of canoodles on a park bench in the twilight of an early spring night, or the hot and filthy, virile dog-fucking of late summer, hips locked together, both bathed in sweat. Or that sudden fucking that comes from the desire to procreate, those tangled desperate fucks which are also seedings, implantations, these shaftings so common amongst the young – up against the railings in an alley behind a pub, skirt up, her legs around his waist, those fuck-me-now moments which keep the planet heaving, spinning.

The idea of a single mate for life is abhorrent to us, an abstinence we don't understand. Most of us would die of boredom and sexual frustration if we were forced to have only one lover, just one for a lifetime. One person to fondle, only one person to satisfy our moods. One lover to carry us through all the ages of our life, to suffer long droughts, or cope with the periods of gluttony, those times of insanity and greed, when we feast on fantasies made real? The idea seems ludicrous, impossible. But most human men and woman aim to adhere to this model of monogamy even though their God-hero Jesus

Christ was no saint; he copulated with that sacred whore Magdalene and many more.

Bill and I kissed and caressed each other on the sofa for what felt like an hour. All the while I whispered loving words in my own soft-smooth language. *I will fuck you and relax you, I will save you from the sadness she has caused you. I don't want you to love me, just fuck me, my one demand, and I will fuck you kindly, lighten your day up – I will return a smile to your lips, I can see you are unhappy, oh I will make you happy.*

Until then I had used my spittle on his cock to lubricate my slow massage. I'd been very careful with him, holding him with the foreskin still covering the shaft, like a purse, only gently pulling it back now and then, using my palm to circle the tip. This brought judders of pleasure. His body convulsed. His eyes rolled backwards. Then, when I felt he could take even more, I pulled back the foreskin and exposed the whole red-raw pink of him. Oh – a majestic phallus, all intense and so, so shy. This was like another introduction of sorts, a coming out of himself, a kind of *hello Miss Lady Pussy.* A man's naked and erect cock is always a shock, a surprise and feast on the eyes. It is why I hunt men. For this great prize, this intimacy. This tender virile offering. What with these teeth of mine it's like offering a juicy shrimp to a catfish.

I plunged my head downwards onto it, holding the foreskin down with one hand, slow-sucking his shaft with my lips all moist and tucked over my teeth. This was another trick I picked up, this from a Jewish harlot in Camden Town, Zohar she was called. Zohar Blumstein. She was a young and lithe Jewess with a neatly trimmed quim who I met at a sex soiree in Angel. I had seen her sucking a man who seemed so utterly transported that I asked her later about her tricks. Zohar showed me and charged me a few quid. I was happy to pay, but not before I sucked her off and showed her my best cuntsuck – and then she gave me the money back.

I licked Bill and sucked and sucked. Up and down I stroked all the while.

Bill groaned. His pupils were dilated. Oh, it's so pleasurable to see a man so sated, to be the giver. I bent to nestle his shaft between my breasts. With my free hand I held his testicles, wanting to put them in my mouth too.

Not those, he said, protectively.

I laughed.

Don't you trust me?

No, he laughed, gently. He'd noticed my teeth.

What sport! I buried my head deeper into his loins, using my hands to milk him as I sucked his cock. I left his jewels alone. Even so, he managed to hang onto his seed. I sucked and caressed and sucked and next thing I knew he'd had as much as he could receive.

Half-naked, his jeans unbuckled, he picked me up whole, carrying me outside to where he worked.

The night was still, watching us, everywhere a million eyes on us. The smells confirmed rain was due; a tang spiked the air, the soil underneath releasing a bitter musk.

Then – oh Lord. Bill's workshop was a dangerous place. Iron all around. Pinned to walls in the form of wheels, in baskets on the floor, in some of the furniture. It made me nervous and unsure but I was loath to stop the flow of our lust. I was somewhat reckless and giddy with my new conquest. I made a mental note: do not touch anything. Or step anywhere without looking first. Iron, to my people, can be fatal. It is the antithesis of what we are, able to eradicate, obliterate. Bill didn't notice my apprehension at all. This was his lair, he had brought me here to fuck, to pleasure me and lose himself. Besides, the element of danger gave me a thrill; I was all the more exhilarated to be there.

Bill slid me onto a long wooden table, laid me on my back, like a feast – and feast he did – kissing the half-moon of my diaphragm, his beard like moss on my skin, a great oak whispering his secrets. His tongue glided over me, his hands tracked the meridians under my skin – oh – he knew about them, delicate ancient tracks. These are the songlines of the skin, designed by angels to release intense ecstasy; they are a map under the flesh. Touch them lightly and the body secretes the sacred chemicals, serotonin, oxytocin, endorphin, the pheromones of lust. He knew these lines and ran his fingertips along them, making the patterns of a river stream all over me, meandering his velvety cock along these tracks – he smiled. Oh, he was a better lover than I could have possibly judged, this man of the woods. Had one of his ancestors been one of us, was there a sprite in his lineage? I writhed under his touch.

Our eyes locked. This was a man with tantric skills; he gazed deep into me and I gazed back, whispering love charms and mantras to Priapus, the God of Cock.

I encouraged him to slide his fingers into me and guided him to my spot, deep inside, where he would find a warm sweet reservoir. Already it threatened to burst. A rivulet sprang from me, tiny, indiscreet, betraying me, dripping from between my legs. Bill held me in his hand, the butt of his palm jammed to my pubic bone, the fingers slowly circling the silky flesh inside me. He stroked me perfectly and I was opening. And no, I wasn't concerned then, that I had found a human match. I had no inkling of any danger that could ensue. I'd forgotten the iron wagon wheels on the wall, the hooks and nails in the baskets on the floor. I had met a man who knew how to make love. I had not been conquered. Far from it. However, I was being met, by a human male – and this was a first.

It was no longer an act on my part, a Sex Magick Seduction, a ritual, one of my many set pieces. I stopped with my tricks. Oh, and I can do many tricks, all right: make my body 'stream' with libidinal forces; this gives men a thrill to behold. Or buck with energy-orgasms. I can suck cock and balls together like the Holy Whore of Babylon, a distant ancestor I believe. I can use the dark forces too, if need be, inflict pain with fire and ice, with soft suede whips and singletails made from bike chains, from bull's tails. I can string my lovers up, keep them hooded, gagged and bound, sellotape their mouths shut, drip wax, run Mummy's best silver forks over a soft rump, take a razor to a ribcage. Oh, my people have been shown how to give pleasure by means of inflicting pain. But these notions of dark Eros, of fanciful circus sex had all dissolved while Bill had me in his hand, while his fingers were slipped inside.

I had never lain under a man before.

But I allowed this.

A mistake.

Bill above me, gazing down. I dripped. And soon, yes, there was a gentle release from deep inside me, my own honey ran from within. My translucent grass-scented cum flowed out of me. Bill swirled and swirled with his fingers and thumb, and sure enough, he had found the right place and down it all came, my own sweet nectar. A release – *ahhhh*. It ran all over his hands, and it fell onto the floor, a small gentle cascade, a splash. I giggled, delighted, and I could sense Bill was a little awed. I looked up at him as I lay there on that wooden table and for a moment it occurred to me that maybe, for a man like this, I could make a more permanent crossing over.

Bill kissed me on the forehead. I kissed his wrist as he kissed me.

Some of my sisters have married men, have left the woodland behind. They are imps. Lilatha-like. Sirens. Witch-like and brazen little whores. They do it for the money, they do it for the trappings of modernity which go with the marriage ceremony: TV, microwave, iPhones. It's never a true match. They opt for hot running water and the Internet, and really I don't blame them. I'm not one to judge. Winters are brutal in the woods. They choose comfort over true compatibility. They choose the material pleasures of the human world and then they teach their lovers the skills they possess; it can be an easy crossover. The departure of an imp woman for the human world has often proved successful up to a point, and there are hundreds, over the centuries, who have made a good enough marriage in the world of men. We have enough in common. The ears and suchlike can be dispatched with or hidden; these days a good plastic surgeon can tuck and nip or remove them if need be. Modern surgeons can humanify a woodland type.

Me? I had, up until then, always resisted this crossing over, despised the limitations of the human world, especially when it comes to my freedom and sexual loving.

Bill was the first man I found a temptation. Bill surpassed all expectations with his presence and his lovemaking. I squirmed and writhed and dripped on that long oak table – while all around me were arranged those trinkets of iron. A kink. I was delighted to be so pleasured in such death-defying circumstances.

Then, everything changed. I was softened and open and Bill had been sucked to hardness beyond measure. We were now hungry for fucking and everything became quick, our hands were everywhere, pulling at clothes, tugging, mouth on mouth, and then we were on the floor.

I was on top of Bill, riding his cock, laughing, enjoying the fit of him. That was another surprise. Only now and then is the fit of cock and cunt ideal. That's when I would judge if a man was good for me. Rare. But with Bill our genitals were designed to fit each other. Of course – long ago – he had been designed for me. His cock slid into me, snug. The girth of it made the friction intense, delivering all the release left stored in my body. I came and came as I rode him, not just one orgasm, but two, three, again and again I thrust myself onto him and he thrust upwards in to me and then – oh – *Jesus*. A bolt of lightning through me, a feeling of being split in two and at the same time soldered shut. Heaven. Perfection in my loins and the Holy God of Fucks up there smiling down. I praised the Lord of Horn, thanked Him for these moments, for my fine body, for the most natural compulsion to copulate. My body sang with ecstasy. And Bill too was lost. I saw the whites of his eyes and oh – we fucked like hornets out there in his shed, hovering, drunk with lust.

And yes, I heard Miss Out-in-the-Cold tiptoe across the courtyard, woken by what she heard, the cries we made. She was aghast and stricken; I could hear the breath catch in her chest. The worst part was that she was also excited by our lust, inflamed with the passion she saw before her eyes. I had ignited her partner like she couldn't and boy did it turn her on. She wanted to join in. Wanted to get involved, to fuck and be fucked in same astounding way, to be pleasured and opened, oh yes. She wanted to find this part of herself, the gentle golden lake which lay secret within her, poor unfucked woman. And I would have welcomed her, then. For I am generous and bisexual enough. I would have enjoyed her cunt, her skin, I would have licked her clean, tickled her up enough for Bill. She could happily join our knot. I had space for her in my cold heart then and in my fickle desire.

But she didn't have the guts. She turned tail, ran back. Her pathetic muffled sobs rang loud across the cobbled yard. I laughed. I forgot about her then and her stupid eggs, her unused sexiness.

*

We slept together in the workshop, on the floor, on a foam mattress Bill had stashed in there along with a million other prizes. He threw some sawdust-speckled blankets over us and we fell asleep curled around each other. Yes, we daemons sleep; we fall willingly into the darklands of the unconscious too. We need our rest, just like the angels and the humans and other creatures, animals, pixies, elves. We demons like to close our eyes and dream. If God is the unconscious, we go to meet him there.

On waking, I was heavy-limbed, in the same position I fell asleep. Bill's beard rested on my shoulder, his body so huge it swept around me. I slipped from this position and left him asleep, picking my crumpled shirt up from the floor, pulling it on. I roamed the workshop carefully, picking amongst the trove he'd amassed. It was all very neat, orderly, and so the piles of iron were easy to avoid. His tools were safely secured in their holsters. I had slept soundly in a trap. Even so, I wandered around, intrigued. The stacks of wood on the floor and up against the wall, pieces he'd salvaged from demolition sites, from rivers, beaches. A stillness in that workshop which reminded me of the woodland in the morning, when the sun is just piercing the topmost branches, dappling the undergrowth.

Again, I felt a resounding empathy with Bill; unexpected and unwelcome – it seized me unawares. He was a great lover, yes. But there was more to him; we had more in common and this commonality made me feel oddly sullen. He was not my usual fuck, not at all like Samael. Bill was a giver.

My usual lover, Samael is the dark prince of the woodland. He and I have fucked for centuries on and off, our lust eternal and, oh yes, he is as much a trickster as I am. He is a malevolent succubus, ugly and handsome and a little insane. But we pleasure each other just fine. Now – this Bill, a lover who pleased me in ways I hadn't understood before. A contrary mixed-up feeling came over me, one of mistrust: I was far away from home and yet at home. I realised I'd stayed too long. This was supposed to be a one-night-stand, a wine-driven lark. I should have taken myself off. I should have left him to sleep. That was my thing, generally. To appear and then disappear. But I felt unaccountably melancholy as I stood there alone in that shed, Bill sleeping: unhappy and also secure. How had I arrived here in this peaceful spot – post-coitus? *Go*, I told myself. *Go now, while he is still aslumber. Skedaddle, go and leave them to each other; they will either split or get over me. Or I will make things better for them, common also. Go and leave before he wakes, go now and kiss him goodbye, kiss his feet as you do with those you've enjoyed. Vanish, vamoose, saunter down the road in your platform heels.*

Also, I was a little turned on. Bill lying there, so vulnerable. A man asleep – what a wonderful sight. I was wearing only my shirt. It was smeared with his cum. It reeked of our loveplay. I perched my bare ass on the wooden table and I opened my lovely legs and I spat on my fingers and began a slow massage, up and down between my thighs and I used him again, the sight of him there to give myself the best damn self-fuck there is in heaven. Oh, I writhed and rubbed and fornicated with my own quim, up and down, stirring the magic energy stored there. Soon, the kundalini rose up in me and I was alone, aglow, watching Bill, frigging myself, my fingers playing the strings of my sex. I writhed and fucked myself so happily as I watched Bill sleep, oh he was lying there, so innocent, and I came over the sight of him, my night hunt, the sight of his back, his rib cage. I came till I squirted my own cum into my hands. And then I rubbed it into my stomach, into my pubic hair. I licked my fingers, pleased with myself. *Good morning.* Good freakin' morning.

*

I didn't leave Bill lying there, as I should. Instead, I was taken with an idea. I ran bare-assed out into the light of day. I knew I'd scared Janey-Wife off, that she had departed, left the house with me in it, the silly prig: the worst thing she could do. I searched the bookshelves for those three stupid eggs, finding them quickly. One made of beech wood, another the egg of some huge bird, all creamy and smooth, an emu or ostrich, the third a beaded box. The bird egg I smashed to pieces on the kitchen floor, sweeping the broken shell carefully onto some old newspaper. The other two eggs I snatched from the shelf as they would also be useful in my charm. I returned to the shed, carrying my ingredients. Bill still lay in his lagoon-shaped way on the mattress, at peace.

I wouldn't disturb him. The eggs and the crushed shell I heaped on the long wooden worktable. From the buckets of wood and heaps of non-iron loot in the workshop I began to construct my own effigy, an edifice I would build around the eggs, a tower. I would bury those eggs once and for good.

In minutes, my charm materialised, a sculpture of infinite surfaces, all stones and glass, and tree parts. All shells and pieces of china plate and shoe horns and smashed up terracotta pots and the soles of rubber sandals I found amongst the buckets of stash. The tower contained all Bill had carefully salvaged from other lives, a tribute to his inner life, to those parts of others he found enchanting. And all the while, as I built higher, I made a picture of who he was and had been until then, for this collected debris was his private diary. I guessed that his Janey-Wife never read it, even though it was left open right there in front of her. I knew Miss Egg Collector had a similar inner diary, her chasm of doubt. Her eggs were a manifestation of all the disappointment she'd kept shored up inside. She had hoped for so much more in life, more than Bill. But mostly, she had wanted more from sex. But she had never foraged, been out there to find it. Most human females don't, to be fair, for they get labelled sluts and sluts in the human realm aren't respected, let alone celebrated as they should be. And so Jane didn't enjoy Bill, not as I had – even for one night. Jealous? Maybe I can admit this now, but it feels unlikely, for jealousy is not an emotion commonly known in our race of polyamorists who share lovers freely. Well, maybe I

was in that moment, maybe I was indeed a little . . .
tetchy. Maybe I didn't even know myself then, my
motives for what I did next.

I hexed them. And hexed them well and good, hexed
them with an irreversible curse. In Bill's private diary I
would bury hers, cancel out these two mismatched lives.
My curse was this:

> For ever more,
> Bill and Queen of the Unfucked Bed
> would, like magnets of the same pole,
> repel each other instead.

I danced around and rubbed the tower with my breasts,
licked and spread cunt juice on it, and swore this oath,
sealing my intention. Oh, I was pleased with myself,
driving these two apart. Little Janey-Prig, she deserved it.
I would have more of Bill, then leave him wanting more
of me.

Soon afterwards, Bill woke up, all sleep-doped and
bewildered. I was on him again, slow and mischievous,
slipping into his waking dream and riding him as he fell
back into half-sleep, rode him like a butterfly on a leaf,
so that he couldn't be sure I was there at all or if I was
real and his head rolled from side to side as he moaned
with pleasure and the narcotic of sleep. I spoke of
daemon-faeries then, told stories he'd heard many times,
recounted them in my tongue: of how we came to be,
how they say we aren't good enough for heaven or bad

enough for hell. How we have claimed our own territory in parts of the world that men are too lazy to look for. I cast a spell on Bill, whispering into his belly hole, into his skin. I licked him like a cat, cleaning him.

Later, when he was coming round, when his eyes opened and he saw me, he panicked for a moment. "Are you real?" he whispered. I nodded and smiled and said "oh yes, very real". I slipped off my shirt to prove it and let him enjoy the sight of me astride him. He relaxed again and my pearl skin shone and my eyes shone too and he writhed under me. "Where have you come from?" he wanted to know. I told him where – even gave him directions, in my language, of course. Bill nodded, as if he'd known all along where to find us. His ancestors knew us, of course they did; his forefathers were all woodsmen, they had come across us. Oh, yes. Bill knew us; we were there, somewhere in his memory bank, in the ink traced in his DNA, he had seen us. The knowledge of us was in his cells.

Later, when I went down on him and took his cock in my throat, again, all of it, boy did that wake him up. Ha ha, a jolt into the world when my wet mouth was on him and my head bobbed back and forth, me, one of the great cocksuckers of the everglades. I continued to pleasure him with single long licks upwards, starting with his warm suede scrotum, then up, along the shaft to the tip. One long good lick with my firm tongue – a feast for me. Bill groaned. Of course, fellatio was once illegal across Europe. Only prostitutes would perform it, which is why prostitutes should be awarded medals rather than shunned by women for whom they kept alive a sacred sexual art. Prostitutes! They are our great sexual mothers. Also, they saved men from fucking cows, from fucking mud. They suck cock like babies suck thumbs, they suck the wounds of men. They are the only women our kind will learn from. For many months I apprenticed myself to Lettice, a tantric-whore of a woman in her 60s, a whore and a mother; six children she'd birthed, all by different fathers, all looked like gods and goddesses, for the fathers had been as handsome as she had been, and still was, beautiful. Lettice lived in Cornwall, a hippie woman who lived in a yurt-turned-pagan-temple in the woods. A whore and a witch and an herbalist she was, and she knew us. We are called piskies in Cornwall and there is much evidence of us there, stone circles and the like, one or two have lingam stones in the centre, still erect, and we like to ride on them and frig ourselves, charge ourselves up. Many of us went to Lettice to learn the art of cocksucking and in return we showed her our tree-cures. As a result the local women, whose men she'd also sucked, many of them at least, whose children she'd cured, let her be. Some of them actually sent their tired, dried up old husbands to her for a good sucking and a fucking. Old Lettice sent them back with a smile.

Oh, I've known many whores throughout my life. Some sacred in their intent, some not so sacred. Not all, but most of them have been interesting women. We all share the same lineage in one way or another: Lilith. She is our root line, our motherage. We all descend from her and even a trace of her lies in every non-whoring female ever sculpted. Earthly whores can spot an imp like me a mile off and we often have many bawdy stories to swap. During that morning with Bill I settled down into a motion I learnt from old Lettice, an act of man worship which would last all morning, me with my gift of rhythm and timing.

BILL

On the cab ride home Lilah's body was pressed close to mine, hips, knees, thighs pressed close, all of us hot in our clothes. I was also aware of an atmosphere: the cab driver shot us looks of curiosity. Lilah was causing it, spreading her musk. A ripe odour wafted the air, from her underarms and from between her legs. From the glands in her neck? She stank – and we swooned, both of us intoxicated. Was she spraying us, just like Choo Choo sprayed the furniture, wetting us down? Whetting her appetite? The cab smelled humid and human, a just-dried scent of exertion, as though we had been out for hours, dancing.

Jane was her usual self. Composed and sitting apart, a little off in one corner, as if she didn't want to touch Lilah. I resented this, I realised; a sense of resentment came upon me now and then with Jane and it came upon me sharply then. Jane didn't like this red-haired woman who had bewitched us both, and I found this irritating. Why bring her home, then? Lilah was half-naked with her short skirt risen up to the top of her thighs. She was smoking and laughing and talking, again about her family in Alabama. By that point, I wasn't listening. I was brooding. I felt annoyed and duped, trapped somehow

– by both of them. And yet I was willing too, I can admit that. I was willing and unwilling, complicit in this arrangement. I wasn't *that* gullible. Lord, no. Something was happening. The women were arranging it. The thing that had been unspoken about between me and Jane was finally being addressed. Sex. The lack of it in our bed. I think I had an inkling of this, yes. I am a man. But not *that* foolish or stupid. The women were up to something.

Me, Lilah, Jane – some trio. Lilah sandwiched right between us. How quickly Lilah had infiltrated us, how easily she'd parted us, had slipped into this unspoken space between us. Was it so apparent to the trained eye? Was the gap between us visible – were we the only ones who couldn't see it? Later, of course, I guessed Jane's fickle plot, what she had cooked up, drunk. Or maybe she had been dreaming up our split long before Lilah arrived, long before that long summer night. But, as things turned out, nothing was simple: I had been picked by Lilah. And Lilah had been picked by Jane. But Jane had completely underestimated Lilah. And the two of them had underestimated me.

*

The cab dropped us off and we filed into the warmth of our house. Immediately, I felt more at ease, on my own territory; the balance of power shifted away from Lilah. This imp-creature was no longer so unsettling, only intriguing. It was all happening so effortlessly. Both women were somehow agreeing, wordlessly, to making it happen. Jane was allowing it; Lilah was sweetly taking the cue. I had a role to play in it and I was playing it, heroically. I wanted to see what would happen to me. How would I benefit? I was a man, twice the size and physical power of this Lilah woman and I knew Jane well. I felt secure in my own home; I was up for it, whatever 'it' was. We were *all* colluding, me and Jane acting out a wordless play between us. It was exciting. I knew I was on the brink of it, wanting whatever it was to happen. We sat round drinking and talking and even though by then I had drunk quite a lot, I was sober. Jane was tired and excused herself rather suddenly and when she vanished everything changed, forever.

Lilah was on me in a moment.

"Let me show you, show you my love. Don't be afraid, my love. I won't bite. Won't hurt you. Relax and enjoy what I am."

Whispers, the sound of her voice like a stream. It was a foreign language but I seemed to understand it. I felt drowsy, and yet turned on. My dick was solid and erect. I held it in my hands, a powerful erection. It was like a talent she had, of playing me, of making me harder with just the sound of her voice. I held myself in my hands and stroked myself and watched her, fascinated.

"Let me give you everything, relax, relax. Let me fuck you into the heavens. I will be good for you, I will make you alive again, make your skin shed itself. I will fuck you into another realm."

I was enthralled. I found myself seduced at first, unable to resist her. I was a little afraid of her too, shaking at first. I saw flashes of something else, a darker creature, elfin, hairy. Sharp milk teeth. Her ears were mesmerising, long and curvy. What was she? Sexy. Yes. That was true, but much too simple an appraisal. Sexual in a way I'd never encountered with women. Cool-skinned but also hot. She emitted a scent that reminded me of wet earth. Her cunt dripped its juice onto me and I rubbed some of this juice onto my cock, and gently pulled at the foreskin, up and down. I smiled and gazed into her eyes all the while, enjoying myself. It was like being with a girl and a whore. She was so sure of herself and gentle with it. Evil and yet tender-soft. I had to stop a smirk forming on my lips; it felt like an act, like she was giving me a well-rehearsed performance. Was she a whore from an Alabama brothel? She had that white-trash streak in her. Or maybe I associate carnal females with a less well-bred kind of woman. Also, the more pretty a woman is, in my experience, the less sexual. Pretty women often don't enjoy sex. They fake their orgasms, and they cannot hold a big cock inside them, or that is the experience I've had, with Jane and with others. Pretty women are too feminine for the hard fuck realm of sex.

And so I was up for Lilah's tricks. I even had a few of my own. Slowly and languorously, I pleasured myself and watched her. I could see she was loving the sight of my cock in my hands, this whore of the woodland. She was as much turned on by me as I was by her. She was relying on her tricks and her undeniable beauty, her charm, and yet I was the stronger magnet in this scenario. I held myself and let her shimmy and dazzle. It was a seduction and this is more than most women have up their sleeves, certainly more than Jane had. And I was so tired, so sick in the heart of the dismal lovemaking with Jane. I sat there with my unused cock in my hands, holding and stroking it. Janey didn't have a thing for cock. I had married a woman who was the pretty type and also refined. She was unreachable. She loved me in a *holy way* she once said to me and this was no consolation. I wanted my wife to suck my cock. But she had never once taken it in her mouth and I had died a hundred deaths through this lack of lust on her part, oh my poor Janey. She didn't love me like that. There was no harlot in her. And Lilah's hands on my cock felt like a joy I hadn't encountered for a long aching chasm of time, years.

"Take this," this Lilah-imp whispered, kissing my throat. "And this – and this."

Lilah was wonderful to watch, her movements were fluid, like something made of glass, a whore and an artist with it. Her flower-petal tongue on me and her satin cream skin, a glint of defiance in her eyes. Flashes of the glade too, dark and pacifying.

She made a big show of opening her crimson blouse and exposing her breasts, an act of theatre. Sure, they were magnificent and I knew it was a test and so I waited and didn't stare. I let her guide me, let her feel she was in control. I am a lover too, after all.

I stroked her breasts and held her face and gazed into her eyes. This was where I came unstuck, this eye-gazing was fatal, for the Lilah-imp had powers I couldn't match. I began to waver, and feel a little lost, as if the magnetism of the earth tugged through me, as though all around me there was tangled undergrowth, or, I was in some wider space, a moorland. The ground beneath me felt wet and black. I sensed a swirling around my head – butterflies! Thousands of violet butterflies danced around me; the air was like crystal. This Lilah creature dripped her cunt juice onto me and it was dewy and syrupy. I don't know how long she sat astride me, dripping, whispering, half-naked, her breasts caressing me. I'd been so, so lonely for this kind of love.

But she'd drugged me. I was drugged on the mantras she was chanting.

It was some kind of spell that imp cast on me. I couldn't move, and yet I experienced a sensation of falling. Lilah's hands caressed hidden places; her lips parted mine and her tongue-kisses somehow felt non-invasive. Like I was kissing her in a dream. For hours? I don't know. Only that I slipped away from my body, letting her do as she wished, and she pleasured me with her hands, with all manner of tricks. She played my cock like a musician plays a violin, stroking the shaft up and down and then executing exquisite juicing movements, then circling her palm on the head; it all sent me to heaven.

Dear God, those moments dwell in me, still pursue me daily. Harmony. Communion with another being, with this unusual woman, a person I didn't know or like or understand. I was scared of Lilah in the pub; I thought she was a pest. And she was a pest, unrelenting in her lovemaking, forceful without using force, cajoling, tempting, irresistible, oh, she knew what she was doing – her movements were agile and invisible.

Lilah was a surprise alright. She was a freak occurrence, an experience I share with a smidgen of humanity, with other men who've come across her like, other poor fucks. Sometimes, I fantasise about placing an advertisement in a national newspaper for other men to come forward. I yearn to meet them, compare their stories to mine. Do they have pictures in their heads, like I do, mesmerising scenes of carnality? Do they feel used? And yet also stirred up by the memories of their nights with such a creature as Lilah? Do they visit libraries, as I do, pore over books, order great leather-bound texts from rare book sections? Do they have marks on their skin, which have never healed properly? Do they sit awake at night, peering out their bedroom windows? I'm not deluded. If a judge or jury were to question Jane carefully about that solstice evening I suspect she'd have made similar observations: Lilah was real.

*

The dead of night, high summer. The kind of temperature before an earth tremor. The air was fragile, taut with lack of moisture. Lilah was half-naked, on top of me. I saw her run her fingers across her lips, as if to seal away those teeth. And then she plunged down on to my naked prick. Her mouth was firm and wet and tender, more agile and juicy than cunt, half oyster, half tiger, working me, milking me and using her hands too, kneading my balls, sucking my cock, her saliva was thick and viscous. Her mouth was more active than a woman's quim, and this kind of sucking will make any man lose reason.

I could feel my cum loosen. She would drain me if I didn't intervene and I wasn't going to let her take whatever she wanted. I pulled her mouth from my crotch and kissed her savagely, saying *stop you little prick tease, just one moment.* I picked her up, bodily, and laid her out on my wooden table, pulled off her denim skirt. I remember her cherry-coloured panties, made from fine silk, trimmed with black lace, a whore's undergarment. I peeled them from her and admired her creamy curves and her auburn tuft. She lay there all surprised. Pleased and ready, too, for a reversal of pleasure. She hadn't expected it.

Lilah lay back, twirling tufts of her red hair, spread out stark naked on my long wooden workshop table. There, really there, and yet also a figurine, a piece of something else, a ship's figurehead, maybe, or a neon motel sign. I knew how to touch her body, the leylines of delight, all there, under the skin. I trailed my fingers and my cock along these lines, danced my prick a little jig, the velvet tip leaking a little, a trail across her luminous skin. Her skin raised up in seizures. Her desire produced a patina of bumps, gooseflesh. A wondrous thing to see a woman so taken with desire, almost enough pleasure in that. In moments like these lust is related to spirit, to Godliness. But Lilah gave me a look from hell. I wondered who she was. It felt so natural to be with her.

I dripped cum all over her stomach and she was dripping too. We hadn't fucked yet. I hadn't entered her, even after all that time. We smiled a lot, laughed too, for this had been lengthy foreplay. I could feel I was weak at my centre, in my sternum and my loins had melted;

my thighs were trembling. I climbed onto the table and slowly sank into her. Then we were fused physically and I faded mentally, whispering to her God knows what. Prayers? Obscenities?

Oh, my Jane, my wife, how I'd missed this with her. Never once had I laid her down like this and clambered on top. Our marriage had been chaste of lust. How? How can a man's life can go by without this language, how can a couple survive without Eros, without these moments, this glue between man and woman? This muffled speech, these shocked gasps. They live in the wood of us, in the thick of us. I was silent for so long, and then, with Lilah, I spoke like a mute speaks, my tongue in knots, spitting out the sound of words which are so rarely spoken, the words for lust.

I slipped my fingers inside Lilah and found her spot, a small spongy raised up area in the wall of her cunt and I pressed it gentle-firm and she writhed and I swirled and circled my forefingers, and before I knew it I had her. She arched her back and gasped all kinds of curses in her language. When we both looked down at her quim we could see that it was glistening with serum and that she had released a small puddle of this liquid onto the table and also the floor. I gazed at her and saw she was undisguised. This raw, she was a creature of immense loveliness, a rarity. Her ears twitched, her face glowed; she was something a billionaire might collect for his private zoo.

And I too, wanted her. I could have kept her held in a crate or a coop. A sex slave for me and Jane. Lilah would have made our marriage happy again. Janey could frig herself quietly every morning and I could have this little imp. All for me, this Lilah who was squelchy inside, a lover to keep me company. I knew I could love this Lilah-imp. I was delighted with her wetness, her lake inside. I was greedy for more of it and my cock was still hard as a tor of granite.

Quickly, we were on the floor and Lilah was on top of me, a fire between us. We clamoured at each other, artless, desperate, fucking like animals, hips locked and our bodies bathed in sweat. Lilah was physically more powerful than she appeared, pinning me down, swallowing my cock inside her. I'm surprised we didn't wake the whole neighbourhood with all the noise we made. We shouted to the rafters, laughed and swore and bit each other and thrashed as we fucked each other. God we fucked like demented teenagers, clambering over my worktable, under it, a tormented and tortuous experience and, God, I loved it. Lilah grinned at me, her eyes gleaming, feral again. The creature at the bar? In all that frenzy, for a few seconds her eyes went dark and her skin faded to a mottled blue-purple. Was I being violated? Was this some kind of sexual attack by a pervert? For those hours I was with Lilah I was released from that world I'd accepted, the dull, kept life of some domestic creature – a husband. I wanted none of it. I was in the wood, on my back, the sap in me risen up. My skin was on fire.

Fragments of that night are still part of me, still live in me. At night I sometimes wake with Lilah on top of me. I am simultaneously admiring of her beauty and cringing with terror, her body moving rhythmically, riding me.

Often I still catch glimpses of that other creature too, another type of face lurched up from a swamp or an underground chamber, most unlovely; a small withered thing, hunchbacked and wart-ridden. I often wake sweating. Confused. Sometimes I take my head in my hands and shake it, trying to knock out the images which haunt me.

I slept heavily. I didn't experience any guilt, didn't think of Jane, or what I'd done, no thoughts of the consequences of those hours in my workshop with Lilah. I slept like a baby, in fact, like I needed to sleep and hadn't slept throughout the years of my divorce and depression. I didn't dream of my first wife, the bitch. I have never dreamt of her. It was a dead man's sleep. A year's sleep in one night. I was tired from sex, from giving and loving and this fatigue was welcome and new, the tiredness of vigorous lovemaking. We curled up on some foam I found in a corner, smattered with wood dust. I fell unconscious, with Lilah's warm body in my arms.

Before falling into unconsciousness I was struck by a strange concern: Choo Choo. Where was he? I hadn't seen him about – and this was odd. Choo Choo liked to sleep in my workshop and liked to greet us when we arrived home. Where was he? I worried about him, fleetingly, that he'd been hurt or trapped somewhere, that Lilah had scared him off. I worried that she'd laid her strong musk all over the house. I would look for Choo Choo the next day, bang his cat bowl with a fork. That always brought the bastard running.

4.
CHOO CHOO

JANE

I woke suddenly. Immediately I was afraid. I knew Bill wasn't next to me before I even checked. Adrenaline flooded my veins. I lay in the dark for several moments. The clock radio next to my bed read 3.21 am. I tried to think clearly: could they be downstairs? Were they still talking? Had Lilah gone? Would I find Bill on the sofa, snoring? I had no notion that my loose and drunken plan had worked. Desperately, I wanted everything back as it was, had always been. I loved Bill: Bill was my heart's true love. I was more than sober. I was in our marital bed, our home. I'd been drunk, full of fantasy: oh, dear God. What had I done?

I groped on the floor, pulling on my jeans, prodding my feet into slippers. Two floors up, but our home carried sound, all those wooden floors. But the house was silent, no sounds from the sitting room below. The lights on the landing were on, as I'd left them. Bill hadn't been up. I descended, practising what I'd say: the game was over. I'd order Lilah to leave immediately. Hold the front door open. Later, Bill and I would talk. I would explain myself, own up to my fantasy life, the faceless men I conjured up. I would finally talk about my drunken father, the way he scared me. I would own up to my demons. I was withdrawn, somehow, from life, from my own sexuality. It wasn't Bill's fault. I needed therapy, perhaps, or maybe we could go see a counsellor together. I would do anything now. I had been foolish with Lilah. What had I been thinking? Bringing another woman home? Our problem must be common, surely? Surely there were other couples like us. Sexually mismatched, but still in loving relationships? Unfulfilled potential, that was my problem. Somewhere I was still a girl. I was ashamed of this and hadn't turned to Bill to explore myself, let alone him. But I *could* find it with Bill; I knew I could. He was there, waiting, and I hadn't come forward. Images flashed before my eyes: Bill and Lilah entwined. Bill and Lilah elated, laughing, a bundle of naked limbs. Bill and Lilah staring coldly at me. Lilah's long and pointed ears.

*

At the top of the final flight of stairs I hovered. The lights below were also on. But still, I couldn't hear them. I tiptoed down.

I peered into the sitting room; it was empty, stifling hot, the windows closed and a fug hung in the air. Whisky and stale cigarette smoke. I had been drunk, numbed, when I had plotted this. My family curse, to drink away the shame of our failures. The long day's heat, the scent of bodies. Signs of them: empty glasses, Bill's shoes thrown off, Lilah's handbag on the sofa. Oh, if only I'd had the presence of mind to go through it, to find out more about her. But I was crazed with fear. Where the fuck were they? Dread stirred in my veins. Were they in one of our spare bedrooms? Had I passed them on the *stairs*?

"Bill?" My voice cracked. "Bill? Where are you?" I was on the verge of tears. I walked towards the dining-kitchen area, half-expecting to see their clothes strewn all over the floor. What had I done? The kitchen was empty too. The lights glared. On the floor, Choo Choo's bowl, his food untouched.

A creak. One of the french windows out to the courtyard swung outwards. In a moment, I guessed. The light was on in Bill's workshop. My breath caught in my chest. I was overcome with an urge to go back upstairs, back to bed, leave them to it. Fear is no guide, I know now. It doesn't tell you what to do, rather it blurs one's judgement and causes confusion. I went to the French windows. The doors of the workshop were closed, though one was ajar, light slicing through it. Light poured from the panel of high windows.

The winters are mild where I come from.
Where had Lilah come from?
Sit in a tub full of ice cubes sometimes.
My heart pounded.
Me and my sinful ways.
How had I let her in?
Storm
Night
These names came to me.

I wanted this Lilah-creature to be gone. I wanted her away, returned back to wherever she'd come from. I was scared. I was an idiot. I would get on my knees, beg Bill for forgiveness.

I slipped out, crossing the courtyard. I heard them first, a sound more disturbing than what I saw. I overheard their cries, Lilah's thin lucid song of orgasm. I stopped, pressing my hands flat to the workshop door. The sound she made struck a chord within me, the sound of ecstasy – peaceful, harmonious. The sound found its way into my bloodstream, my stomach softened. I stood, listening, experiencing a profound sadness, a feeling of shame. I was sorry, sorry for myself, for what I had done. Sorry I hadn't loved Bill the way he deserved to be loved; I hadn't loved him properly.

I overheard Bill too. His moans were different to the ones I knew. He was gasping, delirious. I didn't push the door open, or burst in shouting. I could have bludgeoned Lilah, wanted to, with any one of Bill's tools, a hammer, a mallet, clubbed her with a piece of cherry wood. I could have throttled her with my bare hands there and then. Murder seems like no crime in moments like this, it seems possible, even right, to kill off the enemy. Dark thoughts surged, the most sinister of possibilities. I would smash Lilah's skull, bury her in the garden. Cut her into tiny chunks. Feed her to Choo Choo.

Then I peered through the slit in the door.

Bill was on his back. Naked, spread-eagle, his head arched back. Lilah was on top of him, naked. She rode Bill like a horse, moving rhythmically back and forward, rising and falling onto him. Lilah appeared stronger, muscular, her body luxurious and young, her pearly skin taut and veined with blue. The sight of them inspired an ache: part grief, part response to witnessing such joyous carnality. Part despair too – for this was what I wanted! To be Lilah, then. To be her. To join them, join in. To fuck Bill like she was fucking him. I didn't watch for long; the sight was too strange, too difficult to behold. It wasn't anything like the fantasy I'd conjured of them; it was worse, far worse. My own loins were inflamed, and I was deeply sad and ashamed. Eventually, I backed away, wretched, running back into our house.

*

The second egg was an ostrich egg, huge and creamy and fat. A comedy egg, I found it in an antique shop on Portobello Road. Again, maybe I dreamt things up, imagined lands far off, deserts and tufts of tough grass, antelope and crocs.

We were in a B&B on the north Norfolk coast; we had taken ourselves off on a seaside holiday weekend. Outside the window a flagpole flew the Union Jack. A long pier protruded from the beach out into the pewter sea, at the end of which we had found a bowling alley.

Bill opened the box.

"What's this?"

The egg, all innocence, all snubby cuteness, peeked at him from layers of tissue.

"It's for you. Egg of my heart."

Bill blushed.

A tear rolled down his cheek and I wiped it with my finger.

"You take good care of me," he sighed.

Bill put aside the egg, still in the box, drawing me to him, kissing me all over my mouth and neck and breasts, murmuring declarations of love. I squealed with pleasure and let him do as he wished, loving him, but somehow not quite wanting him like that. We were both like children.

I ponder constantly: is true love is a state of grace? *Agape*, the love that descends from on high, from God, no less. Is this kind of love a blessing? What God uses to make us better people? It feels like this might be possible. Love made me feel innocent. Child-like, even. Most emotions are a reaction to this or that. But my love for Bill was spontaneous and had no motive. Bill was in my heart and he lifted my spirits, made my life better. I loved being around him. He made life feel more original. It was a big, powerful love I had for him. These ideas were part of my private inner life: my diaries and dreams of trips to other continents. I had travelled a lot before meeting Bill, and still had wanderlust. Often I pictured myself on a boat, sailing the Pacific, surviving waterspouts which hurled fish. Or I saw myself crossing a vast rippling desert. Me and my fantasies of escape, and my constant surveillance of the heart, the conundrum I lived within. I loved Bill, but this love didn't contain the element of Eros. I often watched Bill intently, trying to understand my love for him.

Every morning I gazed at Bill while he slept; most mornings I did this first thing. Bill was younger, asleep. Face slack, I could peer further back into his past. Asleep, he was a boy. His large head, his sad face, the sags and creases which had gathered and pulled his face downwards disappeared. Asleep, Bill's face was oval, egg-like, the wrinkles ironed. Asleep, his face was undone, his skin was more supple. His cheeks were plumper. Asleep, Bill was four years old or eight and my heart swelled. I could see the boy he once was. Once, he woke as I gazed at him.

"Good morning," he said drowsily, from the pillow.

"You look peaceful asleep."

"I was dreaming of you."

"While I was watching you dream?"

"I was dreaming you were watching me dream."

I also liked to watch Bill work. The intuition I experienced when I first encountered his workshop echoed in our daily lives. Bill spent many hours in his workshop and often I observed him from the door, absorbed by the task at hand, the possibilities of the wood. Bill, weighing each tool in his palm, humming thoughtfully, divining its use. He pushed a lathe along a rough surface with merciless exactitude, stroking the wood afterwards, as he might stroke the belly of a tree.

I could frighten him easily.

"Bill, cup of tea?"

He never heard. I would enter the workshop, sometimes on tiptoe.

"Bill, love. Tea?" Inches away. No response.

"Bill?"

"Woooaaah!" he would shriek, shooting vertically into the air.

"Dear God, why didn't you call me?"

Bill made furniture on commission and the work was steady. But his creative work, the inventions, they were his real passion: an armchair which was half-bicycle, a dining table suspended from the ceiling. Most of these contraptions were tested on me.

"Darling, come and try this."

"What is it?"

"What do you think it is?"
"I don't know."
"Try sitting on it."
"How?"
"On the seat."
"What seat?"
"Don't be facetious."
"It looks like a big catapult."
"It's a chair. It bounces."
"Why?"
"Why not?"

Bill raided skips by night. He went out late, after midnight, on his bike, bringing home treasure under his coat, or lashed to the handlebars. Often I woke to find a new piece of furniture in the house, a discarded chair or a standard lamp. I knew, like me, that he was casting around, reaching out of himself, that he also had this drive to look for what he needed elsewhere. He was a creative man and without the creativity of Eros between us he buried himself in his work. I had my dreams; he had his workshop.

I also liked to watch Bill cook. We often fought over who would do it. While I was an impatient chef, cleaning up after myself, Bill was patient and messy.

"The main ingredient is love," he often said.

When Bill cooked, the kitchen was in a state of chaos, mashed potato on the floor, cheese sauce bubbling on the hob, fifteen saucepans thrown into every corner, the sink a tower of mixing bowls.

"Honey, dinner's ready," he would announce, strutting into the living room, handing me a plate of penne alla vodka. Once, after TV and a bottle of wine, I collected the plates and took them back to the kitchen. The oven was still on, the door flung wide open. Flames licked out. Choo Choo sat on the countertop, his head buried deep inside the casserole pot. The sink taps were grungy with mash. It was as though Bill had cooked during an emergency, for an army.

Choo Choo. He came with Bill. I married a man – and his cat. He was also an eccentric flatmate. Choo Choo never ran or trotted or walked or prowled or whatever else cats do. He only sauntered, tail up. He was a fat cat, weighing in at fifteen pounds; he had to heave his enormous frame through the cat flap. Sometimes he got stuck. Or he got bored in the process of this manoeuvre, his giant fluffy rear end jutting from the flap, expecting Bill or me to push him through.

Choo Choo spoke in small, enunciated meows. Once he had accepted me, and this took months, he began to use me to get whatever he wanted. He poked and prodded my head if he needed something; often he timed his neediness to whenever I was on the phone. Choo Choo refused tinned cat food. He ate only fish: cod and pilchards in tomato sauce and tuna fish from the can. In the summer, sometimes, he swiped sausages from the neighbours' BBQ. He was a famous neighbourhood tomcat, out every night. Bill loved his huge fluffy balls, couldn't bear to have them cut off.

Choo Choo had even saved a life. I saw it happen from our window. Urban foxes were common in our neighbourhood, mange-ridden, scrawny animals. One began to haunt our neighbour's lawn when they were out; they were unaware of this. One summer afternoon they left their six-month old baby out in her pram. The baby must have been unaccompanied for no more than a few moments when the fox appeared over the wall, sniffing cautiously. I bellowed at it – *shoo* – get away – from our bathroom window. The animal paid no heed. The fox scampered across the lawn, sniffed around the pram, raising itself on its hind legs to peer inside.

"Bill," I shouted.

Choo Choo appeared instead. Fangs bared, on the top of the adjoining garden wall, growling like a dog, the fur on his back like needles. The fox sniffed the pram, undisturbed.

"Get away!" I screamed, half out the window. Snarling, Choo Choo leapt from the wall chasing the larger animal away.

I discovered Bill had secrets too. Stress or unhappiness of any kind often manifested within minutes, hours, physically. Migraines, pains in his hands or knees. Sometimes Bill laughed at this drama, admitting he didn't have arthritis or bone cancer. Or diabetes.

But the panic attacks, when they re-emerged after two years of marriage, frightened him.

"Like a heart attack," he explained.

"What causes them?"

"It doesn't matter what causes them."

"Yes it does."

"When they happen, it doesn't matter why. It feels like I might be about to die."

"Surely it helps to know the cause."

"Not at the time."

I didn't understand.

The panic attacks began when he was splitting up from his ex-wife: chest pains, pains in the heart, sending him running to the doctor, who told him it was all in his head. He controlled them with Beta-blockers and Prozac. After his divorce, Bill's sadness lurked and welled, erupting through his chest. His heart had broken and tremored in the aftermath.

The sex problem with Bill became a constant nagging doubt. What was wrong with me? I wanted to love him physically, but couldn't. I wanted to want Bill but possessed no desire for him. Had I made a huge mistake? Was *agape* too spiritual? I wasn't sure if I didn't want children, or didn't want children with Bill. Each egg I gave Bill made me question this more. I saw the eggs as potent reminders of this failure on my part. I dreamt of eggs, of birth, often seeing myself climbing out of a broken shell. I wondered if I had selected Bill to father me. He was parenting me and that was at the heart of it. Bill was the good father I never had.

*

When I saw Bill and Lilah together, a part of me shut down. I went back to bed and curled up into the foetal position. I cried for hours, not knowing anything, not understanding anything. Later in the morning I got up and dressed quickly. I left the house through the front door, wanting to run away from them, already knowing something had changed forever. Now my home had an atmosphere. I'd underestimated everything and now I didn't know how to get things back.

In a daze, I strap-hung to Angel tube. I worked for a charity, a small close-knit organisation. Luckily, Mondays are busy and no one noticed my anxious face. My desk is in a corner and my computer screen faces a window, affording some cover. I made strong black coffee and switched my computer on, staring at the screen. In it, Lilah and Bill were there – copulating. I heard the sound they made, Lilah's thin joyous song. Lilah, half-cherub, half-daemon, astride my husband, my heart's true love. Bill delirious, lost in her, groaning with pleasure. I couldn't cry any more tears. In fact, my eyes had dried up. A swirling sensation in the arteries, of being on a fairground ride, when you plunge a hundred feet and your innards are sucked upwards. This feeling was constant. I sipped my coffee, unable to concentrate.

The winters are mild where I come from.

Lilah's luscious red lips, her pear-green eyes. The silver bracelets and cheap denim skirt. The crimson shirt, all tied up to expose herself. She was a tart out on the pull only the night before – and now she was in my home. Her smell, like peat or something heavy and fruit-damp. Decayed plums? Lilah, the Hilly Billy, the bumpkin. Those long slim ears, I tried to think of what they reminded me of. Her height too; she was short and yet a fully mature woman. Her sharpish teeth, the flashes of something else. Some kind of animal in her, I had also seen that. Those ears. I closed my eyes and saw her again. I saw her in the pub, the pyramid of peanuts. I saw her in the cab, then the way she high-stepped the lavender down the path to our house. Her casualness, a kind of confidence. Something she knew about us, like she had picked *us* up. Not the other way around. Something about her was an act; she had used us. She knew she could. A sexual trickster, oh yes. A prostitute with blackmail in mind? No. Not quite that. She'd been on the hunt, yes. Midsummer. But I had a hunch, a very odd one . . . from nowhere it came to me.

I did a Google search: pixie, imp, elf. Initially, I came across the usual rubbish, but a deeper trawl took me to the right sites. You can find what you need to find on the Internet; but you need to turn left, onto the dark web. It takes the right software, then the right search engines. Anyone with a bit of hacker knowledge can get to it and then the *otherworld* is all there to trawl: assassins, drugs, guns, and yes . . . imps, elves, spirits from the underworld. I read for hours; read of sightings of faeries and fantasy creatures, all over the world. Russia, Europe, Africa, Mexico, the Caribbean. Trinidadians called them *soucouyants,* the Arabs called them *djins.* They were aggressive and conniving and yes, I found online testimonials, accounts verifying their existence. Deaths, accidents, baby snatchings. But nothing in the mainstream media or print, in national newspapers; no reports of sightings which made headlines in the real world, and no people claiming they'd had similar experiences to me and Bill. No modern-ancient whores pestering or seducing couples.

I read for most of that morning on the dark side of the web, taking care my colleagues couldn't see. I read about edge-lands and liminal spaces, blind spots all over the world, geographical oases, off the grid, where these creatures made their camps. I read of their hexes, that some could last generations, could curse an entire family tree. In Nordic countries imps and pixies are taken seriously. Housing planning officers show them respect when building roads and towns. I read that these creatures could be easily eliminated, killed with iron. They were fatally allergic to it. Was I going mad . . . was my home invaded by an imp? An audacious changeling? Was Lilah a very real creature from tales supposedly made up by once-illiterate housewives? If so, I wanted to know why had those tales been mocked? Like alchemy and astrology, had these creatures been rejected after the Age of Enlightenment? Had they been consigned to myth, ridiculed as "stories"? I wondered if they were only visible to certain people, if there was some kind of half-breeding or leftover lineage which could be traced back to the dawn of man. Lilah had come for Bill, not for me. She had sniffed him out, maybe even accidentally. Had Bill some dim imprint left in him of these *other* people?

Something had gone badly wrong. I wanted to ring Bill immediately, call him back to me. Then it occurred to me – Sebastian. Yes, there was Sebastian, an actual *witness*. He'd met Lilah last night too. Lilah was young and also old. She was some kind of . . . possibility which had materialised . . . something I had wanted to come our way . . . from where? From my imagination? Had I called forth Temptation? I thought about the Ladies, my conversation-with-self. I had made a decision then, to pick up Lilah. A reckless idea; had she drawn it out of me? Was Lilah an actualised *djinni,* conjured up from a part of me? Be careful what you wish for. *Kaboom,* had I rubbed a lamp? I found it hard to think of Lilah without blanking out, as if trying to recall her emptied my mind of thought.

*

Luckily, I didn't have much work to do, no meetings with colleagues or appointments with clients. I closed down the search engines, pushed paper around my desk until lunchtime, head down. At 1pm I slipped out and floated the length of Upper Street to Highbury Corner and into Highbury Fields behind. On a bench I sat with my handbag clutched to my lap, the hot summer sun on my cheeks. I looked at my watch and counted: it was just over twelve hours since we had met Lilah.

I rounded on myself. I was a chronic dreamer. A dreamer since childhood, the habit worsened through adolescence. I was still a dreamer through my twenties and thirties. If you dream, you know what you want; if you dream, you can get what you want. I loved my dreams, couldn't live without them. I have used them to live, to get from A to B. I have lived some of my dreams. I have travelled, made good of myself. Dreams can change things. They are where secret intentions lie. But it seemed like now my dreams had turned real. They had manifested into Lilah. Lilah was what I had been trying to hide, what had been bothering me. Her Type – Whore. I had never been a mother. But had I ever been a woman like Lilah? I was heartsick. My husband had just fucked another woman and I had watched, driven him to it, led her to him. I had underestimated the strength of my love for my husband. Had I really wanted to *leave* Bill?

And then what?

Yes, exactly what?

Dance into the arms of other men?

Approach the men I dreamt of?

Yes. That was what I had wanted. I'd wanted those fantasy men, I'd been naïve. I thought those other men could release me. I could be a more sexual woman with these fantasy men.

Midsummer, in one drunken and dream-fuelled moment I thought I wanted sexual freedom. I wanted a chance to get the sex I wanted elsewhere. And so I lured Bill into adultery. I'd made Bill the reason for my unrest and Lilah the tool of my release. I pictured I'd leave Bill. I set up the excuse. I didn't blame Bill for anything, I didn't see him as the reason for my sexual failure with him. I needed to be gone. I needed the experience and adventure of sexual pleasure. We both needed this part of ourselves. We weren't lovers together. Bill fathered me. I mothered him too, through his panic attacks. It was best, somehow, if we separated, if I left him to Lilah. That had been my line of thinking the night before. Oh, *God.* I was miserable. I never wanted to live without Bill. My love *was* passionate. Bill was my home, my twinned universe. I was far from safe, from comfortable, benign, happy, good. I was sick with fear. In such a vulnerable state, I found thinking of Bill made me feel aroused.

*

I walked back up Upper Street with a lighter heart. I knew I was prepared to do whatever was necessary to correct my mistake. I had a lot of explaining to do to Bill.

In my haste to leave I'd left my iPhone in our bedroom. At a phone box a few metres from the office I stopped. My chest fluttered as I found the coins. I wanted to see if Bill would meet me, explain I needed to talk. Tell him I wanted to be with him. I assumed he wouldn't know I'd seen him with Lilah on the workshop floor. I assumed he would be suffering from guilt, that, like me, he'd had an awful morning. Maybe he had been thinking the same thoughts as me, working things out. Had Lilah shifted something? Our old dynamic. I was sure he'd want to meet up. My darling Bill would want me back. He would come flying to greet me. We would leap into each other's arms. My love, my dearest love. It came to me that we should meet in the same pub we had encountered Lilah. I should revisit the scene of my crime.

The coins slipped in and I held my breath. One, two, three, four, five rings. My heart plummeted. The call minder message on our landline ran, my voice, me asking the caller to leave a message, my tone self-assured, casual.

"B . . . Bill," I tried to speak clearly. "Bill, if you're there pick up the phone." I waited. "Bill, can you meet me later? . . . I'm . . . I need to talk to you . . . about last night. I need to talk about Lilah. I'll be at the same pub we were at. At 7 o' clock. Can you be there? I . . . " but the answerphone message ran out.

I stepped from the phone box feeling stronger. Bill would get the message and come. I knew he would. Already I could sense my life beginning to swing back into position. A better life. We would discuss what happened. I would tell him I had seen them together and it was okay. I experienced a surge of optimism, an intuition all would be well, that, in all this, honesty would prevail. I was still troubled, but much less anxious. Things between us were different now. After all, my plan had worked. Lilah had been the agent for change in our marriage, a catalyst, whoever she was. I went back to work and spent the afternoon answering emails and phone calls as best I could. At six I left and headed across town to the bar where we met Lilah.

LILAH

We surfaced around midday, ravenous. Bill decided to go to the shops to buy lunch. I explained my predilection for sweet food – honey, fruit and the like – and my passion for dairy products. He found this amusing, what most human women avoid. He disappeared with a thoughtful smile on his face. It was then, as I stood with the fridge door open when Bill was gone, that the large ginger tomcat strolled in, hissed and spat at me. I glared and hissed back. Usually this is enough. I stamped my foot and whispered a curse. But the cat growled in response. I closed the fridge door and dropped to the floor; I could smell it had been out rutting. We had that in common. Cats are a nuisance; they show me up. Killing babies is my speciality, oh – a joy to smother an infant in his crib. Cats I rarely bother with.

"Get out of here", I hissed in my language.

The cat's fur rose into spikes. Its ears were laid flat back on its head. It was part-daemon then, an aggressive tom, and I could see it hadn't been snipped; its wildness was still there. The cat stood on its toes, back arched. Most cats won't try to fight, most will spit a little and then disappear. They realise, quickly, they're up against a far bigger animal. But this creature was more territorial than the average domestic cat. It leapt up onto the kitchen table and hissed again, fangs bared. In a moment, I was on the kitchen table too, then I had the animal by the scruff of the neck, howling and screeching and scratching at my arms, dangling, writhing. I shook it hard. The beast screeched even louder.

"Fight, my evil furry foe," I snarled.

The creature sank its teeth into my forearm.

I hissed and swore in my language.

The animal shook its head, and sunk its teeth deeper. Blood seeped and the animal raged. Then I had him by the tail. I yanked him from my arm with my other hand and this was painful. I could have wrung the beast out, broken its back in half. I held the animal by the tail, upside down, and swore at it. It continued to hiss and claw the air.

"Ha, not so happy now, eh, what shall I do with you?"

The cat frothed.

There are many other ways to dispatch with a cat, especially in a kitchen. Knives, graters, grinders, pepper and salt, oil, vinegar. Rolling pins and mallets. I could club the animal and hide the corpse. I could pour olive oil down its throat, drown it. Or I could stick it in the microwave and watch. Instead, I ran with it up to the top floor of the house, the cat struggling as it swung from its tail. I found the bathroom up there, in it an airing cupboard next to a boiler – perfect.

And then I did what I am good at – I pressed my thumbs down slowly, slowly on its throat, watching its eyes bulge, using both hands, gripping the creature hard, crunching its neck cord. Its fight began to lessen and a jet of warm urine fell, *oh*, I could have licked those furry balls, I could have feasted on the thing. I kept squeezing until the cat's head lolled and the body became limp in my hands. Its heart, though, was still beating, *thumpety thump*. A swift screwing action and a flick and its neck was broken. *Ha* – I have earnt all of my names, especially this one, *strangler*. When it was truly dead, toast, kaput, over, I kissed its furry head and threw it like a toy into the cupboard. No Bill or Janey-Tits would look for it there. I left the thing to rot and said good riddance. In the kitchen I dabbed my wound and spat on the tiny puncture holes, the spit an anaesthetic, healing the wounds in an instant.

Bill returned with bulging shopping bags – smiling. As yet the subject of The Wife hadn't arisen. He was in a dream, post-coital, groggy in the head, not-all-there, not-wanting-to-ask-questions, not caring even. I think he even knew he was changing the course of his life. Yes, he was in on it, by then. He had surrendered to the events. He was acting out his part in the honey trap. He had been a willing captive. Whatever had been the big old elephant in the room between him and Wifeykins had now gone rogue. I was interested to see this new mood. Bill was digesting the honesty of his actions, a little wordless, a little overwhelmed. And, almost constantly erect.

Me? Was I 'falling in love' with Bill at that moment, was I? I couldn't tell, for I don't know what human love is. We are loving but not romantic creatures, we don't get too personal with each other in the way of humans. We are far more pragmatic. More solitary, just like that cat of his. I felt different, yes, maybe even unwell. And yet I couldn't leave. It was past midday and I hadn't fled. I'd stayed on much too late. I was *enjoying* Bill's company, his presence. I was glad when he returned from the shop. I wanted him, wanted to share what he'd foraged for.

*

Before lunch we had sex again on the kitchen floor. Quickly, this time, me riding him. Oh, I like to be on top, to be the *domina,* the one who hostesses the show, who stages all the stunts with human males. I am the party thrower, the orgy mistress. I gave him a good fuck, massaging his cock with the muscles of my cunt, and the energy of him rose upwards through me and lit me up. This Bill was made to fit me and I was made to fit him; somehow I'd stumbled across him, this Adam. At first glance he was just a primary model: Husband, Father, the Average White English Male. *Homme Vanille.* Marks and Spencer Man. Nothing remarkable. Nicely castrated by the middle class feminists, cured of any alpha tendencies. He had been trained not to be dominant. Isn't that what feminism has done, it has laughed the alpha males out of town. *Masculinity is in crisis*, say the clever ones these days. Feminism equalised women in the workplace and put men in the shed, where I found Bill. The male alpha doms went underground, thousands of them, to Internet fetish sites and their private dungeons and the like. There, many of my sistren operate, daemon-killers like me. Professional Dommes. Strangulators, ball kickers. Experts in humiliation, bestiality, fucking men up the ass with their strap-ons. Torturing testicles till they turn blue. We Lilatha exist in the shadows, in the twilight; we are around if you look for us. Many men do, those who like to submit. And they keep quiet when they find us. Few imps, like me, stalk the pavements in full view. That's my kink, to fuck The Innocents, men like Bill. I like to dominate Mr Everyday.

And yet, as I had happily discovered, Bill had secret charms and abilities after all. My assessment had been wrong. I rode Bill hard, forging a twinned ecstasy between us. We groaned and writhed, both of us dying afterwards. I laughed with glee, at how Bill gasped for breath. "You're lovely," he gasped. I licked my fingers, tasting his bitter-salt cum. "So are you," I winked. "Feed me now, I'm starving."

Lunch was delicious and replenishing. We fell on fruit and gooey chocolate cake and ice cream and opened a bottle of red wine. I put on one of his vinyl jazz records and danced around naked. *I'll stay one more hour, I told myself. One more hour, just one. Janey-Wife has gone, this house is mine and we still want to fuck. I am not yet sated.* Greedy thing I was, greedy for his cock. Bill couldn't keep his eyes off me, he was entangled – miserably unsure of himself. Distant and yet high on that fuck-chemical of serotonin. It was coursing through him. It was like watching a new drug addict and any minute I might have to catch him from slumping to the floor. He was lust-drunk. But I wasn't. I'd provoked this altered state in men many times before; I had left many husbands in this condition. Usually I fled well before this point. But I was still enjoying myself, still very much the sprite.

I danced naked for a while. Human men love to watch women dance in the nude and very few modern human women do. It is a dead art, relegated to the dim caverns and glossy tables of the lap dancing club. Burlesque strip-joints. Once, it was an art of the courtly harem and the well-paid hetaera; once it was part of Bohemia, of a social stratum of free thinkers and free lovers. Men have danced naked too, for women and other men. There is a long tradition of the Lust Arts. I find this an omission on the part of modern womankind as naked dancing puts men in a state of awe and gratitude. The Wife won't do it, never did. Oh, human women divide their nature. Mother. Wife. Whore. They do not integrate. Good girls and bad. Few celebrate that they are both. So there I was rubbing myself and licking my lips, caressing my breasts, my hips, sliding my hand down between my legs. It was an act, a naked tease. This was one of my many carnival tricks. I have worked in burlesque clubs, learnt the art of grinding and wriggling, stripping off stockings, gloves. Doing what American strippers call 'ass work', removing strings of pearls from my pussy. I have a strong muscular vagina, able to pulse and milk my men. But I do not possess the agility of hookers in the bars and lap dancing clubs of the Orient. I cannot shoot ping-pong balls across the room. I surprised Bill with three small but succulent beetroot I had found in the fridge, already peeled and boiled. I dripped the purple ink over my quim, inserting them one by one, dancing them up and in. He laughed out loud and clapped for me and I took a bow. He knelt for me and ate as I released each soft warm beet into his mouth.

More, he whispered.

And I complied, oh, with cucumbers and carrots and the like. Bill was rock hard throughout. I loved his cock, thick and uncircumcised. The tip glistened. At one point, I knelt in front of Bill and took his balls into my mouth and swirled them round. He trusted me more with his jewels this time. He poured wine over my face and I drank and sucked and his cock was huge and solid and he stroked himself and dripped cum over my face, rubbed it into my hair. Then he was sitting on a counter top, his jeans unbuckled, his thighs bare, his cock like a tower. Me on tiptoe, with my mouth all over him, my head bobbing, all the while kneading his scrotum and his hand reaching down, stroking me, catching the drips. Then, his body juddered, as if Aphrodite herself was stroking the kundalini up from his genitals and up his back. His cum flew in hot spurts, white and pearly, splattering his stomach, the fruit bowl, everywhere. And I came too, my cum cascaded like a torrent to the floor, not a cupful, as usual, but a warm wave fell from that secret reservoir. Like I had urinated, except it was translucent and salt-sweet to taste. And with this release, I began to feel altered. *I shouldn't be here; I should have left.* Bill reached down and cupped the small of my back as I shuddered. My orgasm swamped us both. I looked up at Bill and saw his eyes glittering. *Oh Christ,* he whispered. I could see that he had recognised me. I was Wife No 1. My cover was blown. It was then I whispered my real name to him in my language and he nodded.

The phone rang: loud, piercing bleats. At that point we were lying, spent, on the kitchen floor. My pussy was still swollen and pulsing with joy, my head was still light. *I must go now, must go.* I pushed Bill a little away from me. "It's your wife," I said. Bill stared across at the phone in the hall as it rang. He got up and walked towards it, naked. He bent over it, not wanting to touch it. It continued to ring but he didn't answer it. How could he? I had hexed him well and good. Then we could both hear her voice on the answerphone speaker. Her pathetic, frightened, penitent voice. Bill looked sorrowful. His face was still lit with the perspiration of our lovemaking. But he wasn't moved by the sound of her voice.

"Bill? Bill?"

"Can you meet me at the bar?"

"Can we talk?"

"Bill, Bill?"

Too late Miss What-Have-I-Done. Much too late.

Bill looked pasty. He turned and watched me closely, lying there on the floor, in a pool of my own cum, my quim coloured inky-purple, my face smeared with red wine, with his cum. When was the last time, if ever, he'd had this much fun?

"You're a pest," he said gently.

"Why, thank you." I smiled.

"You will ruin me."

"Don't be so dramatic."

"Will my wife ever come back to me?"

"I'm afraid not." The hex, his cat neatly dispatched. Bill was doomed. I parted my legs a little.

Bill nodded, slowly, as if he understood.

"Come here to me," I beckoned and began to rub myself, rubbing the lamp between my legs, allowing Bill to position himself on top of me, like Adam had tried, and failed, allowing him to hover above, dominate; with a slow nod, *yes, my love, come.* I would leave soon, I told myself. I was still in control. He returned back to the floor which was strewn with our sex; slowly he drove himself in to me, hard and firm, and boy was that one cosmic fuck.

Later, I took him on a tour of all the spots where he'd never had sex in that cold, damp unfucked house. On the stairs, over the banister, on every floor in every room, in the shower. And I loved it all: yes, I was in love then, if that's what it's called. I was in the throes of a love I had never experienced before, not with a man or even with one of our kind. This was a unique coupling, the two of us designed for one another. Cock and cunt united in rhythm, humming together, vibrating, juicing, stirring up the divine ecstasy of the cosmos, spinning joy from the air. We barely spoke, just fucked and laughed and stared and played with each other, delighted in each other's company. I didn't even suspect the danger I was in, that this was what I was on Earth for, this time, this danger, this potential, my potential, fully explored, another dimension of myself exposed. Love. I knew nothing of it till then. It made me weak and unhappy and happy. It made me feel elated and expanded. Better than myself. I felt like I had suddenly grown. I had heard much mention of Love, an emotion. Till then it was abstract, something humans talked about a lot. It was like a piece of news, an event far off which others experienced in the human realm. Now, I was experiencing it and I had a keen sense of its value and intent. It was natural and related to nature and I had seen something similar in the way animals tended their young. I knew about a universal force which existed in a divine form; it was everywhere and very evident in the woodland. And yet this Love was altogether different inside me now. It was very, very . . . personal. It felt like a gift, a new me, a type of grace handed to me – and also I felt mocked. Somehow, betrayed. It had crept up on me, this feeling, exposing me. I felt joyous and I felt guilty too. Is this what the Good Angels, the so-called higher spirits, spread about? If so, I felt alarmed. I was at war with myself, cursing myself for losing sight of my plan, the same plan which always worked in the human realm. Hit and run.

*

Much later in the day, late afternoon, while Bill was sleeping, I towelled myself dry in front of Janey-Wife's wardrobe mirror, inspecting my body, pleasantly marked here and there with Bill's lust, a mauve thumb mark on my breast, a pink rosette on my buttock, a bite mark on my thigh. I rubbed Janey-Wife's creams and potions into my skin, Clarins, Dr Hauschka, Ortigia, loving myself and who I was and what I'd done. Apparently, I was in the act of loving a man. I loved my cunt and inspected it closely. Yes, it was a pretty quim; *it has character*, one of my human lovers once said. My clitoris is quite meaty, hidden under a hood of skin. It swells nicely when I am aroused, to the size of a pistachio nut. My inner and outer lips are discreet, tiny, like wings. And my G-spot is a small sponge, just inside the entrance. I found some almond oil amongst her bathroom things and massaged it through my dark copper tufts, into the folds of my lips. We do not smell like women; we smell very different, like petrichor, that dense muddy scent of minerals mixed up after a rain shower.

I was pleased with myself then. I was tired too; happy tired and sore. I didn't heed my doubts enough. I put them off; I stored them under a file called 'review later'. Surrender? I had been nowhere near. In the mirror I sparkled and radiated evil. I was lit up by all the loving horrors of my deeds. In twenty-four hours I had wrecked a couple's life together. I was massaging her potions into my bush. Oh, I was pleased with my work. And it wasn't quite over.

I left Bill asleep on the marital bed, leaving a note to say I'd be back, that I'd gone to see his wife in the pub where we met. I would go instead of him, explain to her firmly and calmly that she was never returning to her old life. I'd done her the favour she requested of me; she got exactly what she wanted. Her fickle back-to-front plan had worked; she was released from her old constraints. She could now go off and fulfil all her fantasies. She was free of Bill, free to go, disappear. She could now fuck all those men she'd dreamt of fucking. Good for her, little Sex Kitten-in-Waiting – I had done my job. She was released from her unfucked bed.

BILL

I was too scared to open my eyes. To wake to the next day, to what I'd done, to remember it and – good God – speak to Lilah. I didn't want to think of what had happened between us, let alone what to do about it all. How would I get rid of Lilah? I wanted her gone. I wanted to ring Jane. I wanted to run away. I woke panicked, paralysed with fear and regret. Squinting, I realised Lilah wasn't next to me. Had she left, disappeared? Thank God. I prayed she had. Then, my heart sank, I was aware of Lilah – to my right, above my head, her movements furtive and precise, as though with the knowledge she wasn't being observed. She was fashioning a sculpture on my workshop table, a tower of some sort, from objects in the baskets on the floor. A rubber mudguard poked here, half a china plate tucked in there, an old mirror flashed between the two. Immediately I was more alert, hiding my gaze from under the blanket.

Half-naked from the midriff down – the image of Lilah then is etched in my memory: her magnificent skin, her buttocks outlined by the morning's first light, the dark copper pelt nestling between her legs. An unexpected tenderness came on me, a yearning I've carried with me all my adult life. To love openly and to be loved in return. I had given up on this expectation in the second act of my life. It was an ideal of my youth. But then I felt a clear and perfect empathy for this small red-haired woman I'd only just met. In my workroom, phosphorescent with dawn light, microbes like stars spiralling about her as she worked, I swear I saw a being so like those you see in books of faeries and other sprites. She was some kind of halfling: half-woman and half-tree. Or half-child and half-flower. I wasn't sure just who or what she was. Lilah was sexual and yet innocent building that tower to God knows what. It reminded me of the pyramid she had made the night before, of peanuts. Was it some kind of charm? I couldn't guess. I only delighted in watching her, her naked creamy buttocks, my cock growing stiff. I reached down to hold myself and watch her make this sculpture. My fear of her faded. I was in my studio, a space where I was intimate and creative with myself. It was like watching another artist immersed in the creative flow. I didn't want her to go after all.

The curve of her belly, that tuft of copper hair. I experienced a strong pull towards Lilah then, an affinity. We were alike in ways I couldn't fathom. She was a person of the woodland. A lover I knew from another life? She was nothing like Jane, or my first wife. She was smaller, much smaller, wily, and intuitive. She took the lead. I was mesmerised by her creation, by her nakedness, a phallus growing in her hands. I tried to remember the night before, how we'd met her in the bar. I had been fearful then. It felt like months ago, like

Lilah had been here for some time. Like she had moved in. I groaned as I pleasured myself, grasping the shaft of my cock, moving my closed hand slowly up and down, oh, I had never managed to openly pleasure myself in front of Jane. I watched her nakedness and the way she sculpted something from the piles I had collected. I saw her pick up a small stone; I had found it on a beach in Wales. It was deep grey and striped with white lines. She put it in her mouth as if to savour it, and then she rubbed herself on it, quietly frigging the cool stone, her back arching at the pleasure she was giving herself. She inserted the stone and revolved her naked buttocks, happily, and I had a sense of her then, how innocent sex was to her, how she might go about a brook in the woodland, seeing sex everywhere, the possibility to pleasure herself with anything. She had the stone inside her and was swivelling it around, dancing it. She had no idea she was being observed. I loved her then. I loved this sex play; it was a form of magic. Then I watched her remove the stone and place it inside the tower she was building.

Lilah turned.

We gazed at each other for a long moment. Then she was on me and again I was doped with her rained-earth scent and when she removed her shirt I gasped. My cock was hard in my hands. Lilah laughed and plunged her mouth down on to it, her head nestling into my groin and I rested my hand on it, loving her then. As I was beginning to lose myself; she switched from her mouth to her cunt, sitting astride me and fuck me she did, sweetly and with lusty intent and pleasure, enjoying herself. I slipped in and out of consciousness, and half-remember what I saw: her face alight and smiling down, laughing and enjoying the giving. Behind her, the sculpture loomed and disappeared then loomed. I had a premonition then, of my old life coming to an end. I saw myself walking down a long narrow alleyway, alone. I was whistling a tune.

We slept again and woke hungry and full. I hadn't slept or fucked so heavily and perfectly in years. Lilah wanted fine treats: cake and honey and wine and milk, butter and eggs and dark chocolate. And so I pulled on my jeans and found a T-shirt, and left the house for the shops around the block. As I stepped out into the midday sun, I was self-conscious. Had the neighbours heard? Had they seen Lilah arrive? Jane depart? Did they hear our lustful thrashing in the workshop? Had they guessed something was going on – ruction, catastrophe, catharsis next door? Jane must have slipped away; had she found us? Seen us asleep on the mattress on the floor? Would I find a note from her later in our bedroom? Had she fled? Or was there a chance she'd seen nothing at all? I doubted that very much; in fact I realised fully, then, that this had all been Jane's idea. I didn't know what to make of what was happening. I was out of myself, out of my body.

I floated out onto the street, my limbs heavy, my head drowsy with the sex I'd just had. My skin smelled of Lilah, my fingers, my hair. A smell like wheatgrass. Could others smell her on me too? My skin had somehow contracted overnight. It felt tight to my bones, snug, like

I had been washed and had shrunk a little. I tugged at my sleeves, looking about guiltily.

*

In our corner shop I skulked with my basket, picking out the items Lilah had asked for, finding I had a similar appetite for sweet and buttery food. Strange, I don't have a sweet tooth. But I was overcome with a ravenous hunger for honey and soft fruit, pears, cherries, and a fresh white loaf and milk and sugary shortbread. I filled my basket without knowing what I took. The Turkish men behind the counter grinned, nodding with appreciation. As though this was what their wives encouraged them to feed on. A sudden pang: a world of riches out there, dark, forbidden delicacies, everywhere. Other men knew of them. With Jane and my first wife too, I had lived without excess. I had taken my life's pleasures in small and measured doses. I had been a good husband, loyal, yet reined in. This is why I hadn't been able to cut the balls off Choo Choo. He was wild. I was tamed. To my basket I added a bottle of Moët, a bottle of Jack Daniels and a good Merlot. Never had I bought alcohol with such lascivious intent in the middle of the day. I had lived a life of moderation. Jane had a guilt about alcohol; she drank hard now and then; other times she wouldn't touch a drop. I had felt watched, judged when drinking.

We spread the picnic out on the kitchen table, eating with our hands, guzzling champagne from the bottle, honey dripping from our chins. I hung cherries on Lilah's ears and they dangled against her hair and neck. Her ears were astonishing, like dock leaves, tapered and svelte, plainly part of who she was. I loved her ears. I didn't question her about them, but her green eyes flashed and she noticed me looking and I think she was even daring me to ask.

After eating we had sex, quick furtive fucking and as I thrust in to her I sensed a change in her mood, like she was assessing me. Again, I was her experiment and as I thrust, I knew there was danger and something else – the love chemical, oxytocin – it was working its wonders on her. I could see she was softer and yet still trying to remain cut off. I even liked to see this conflict in her, to watch her border on succumbing. I loved her then. After fucking we dozed a little, limbs entwined.

Later, we ate again. I opened the bottle of red wine. Lilah danced around to some jazz, half-naked and honey-fingered. I sat back holding my cock and watched her shimmy round the kitchen, never wanting to leave the house again. I had been living in that house for much of my life. First as a boy, then, later in life, as a man. My mother left it to me in her will. I restored it slowly and built the shed outside. But I'd never shaken the feeling that it had been my mother's home. My father had died leaving her widowed and bereft for twenty years. It had a feeling about it, of loss, of a life unlived. It was where I had recovered from my divorce. Here I had suffered and survived my depression.

In those post-divorce days I was unable to get it up. I would try coaxing a hard on, but often gave up. It was as though every part of my body was depressed, including my prick. Then I met Jane – I guess by then I was grateful, for her companionship and her beauty. Quite quickly, Jane moved in and the house became more hers than mine. I lived in my shed. I had never ever wanted to admit it, but I'd felt a deep feeling of dread in that house. It reeked of despair: my mother's, Jane's and mine. That was why I had bought Choo Choo as a kitten. I needed another male about the place; I needed a companion.

I continued to watch Lilah. A full-bodied lust blossomed in me, wanting to pull her close, penetrate her deeply, fuck her again, there and then across the table, bend her over, spread her legs, lose myself inside her. But Lilah tantalised, undulating just away from my grasp. Her ripe breasts, the curve of her buttocks; she played with herself and laughed and writhed and I knew she had tricks up her sleeve, this Lilah-imp. She had been a showgirl once, perhaps. Or she'd performed sex acts on stage. I watched her wriggle her hips and thrust forward her breasts. Oh, and then she opened the fridge; in it there were some cold wet beetroot. These she slipped inside herself – and danced about.

"Ahh, they feel so cool inside," Lilah gasped. "I've been overheatin'."

I was happy and sad. I ate them from her cunt and yes, it was about then that I was lost.

Then she had my cock in her mouth, me up on the countertop, my jeans down by my ankles. I cupped her cunt, catching the drips. Her head bobbed and I rested one hand on her silky hair; with my other hand, I stroked her. She was pleasuring me and I was pleasuring her and we were both in time with each other, my knuckles kneading her so she had swelled. And then I could feel the results of her sucking, I was about to release myself and quickly I came in spurts, all liquid gold all over me and her. And at the same time I was kneading her soft wet cunt and she also came, fluidly, like an ocean, a wave of warm liquid fell from her and she shuddered and gasped. The floor was slick with her orgasm, and she was shuddering. She was like an animal, naked and glowing and alert and she was also surprised. We both were, her liquid orgasm all over the floor. I held her close in my arms and her body quaked from the release. She had opened me. And I had opened her.

I tried to think. But I couldn't, couldn't clear my head. I could only marvel at Lilah and imagine more carnal scenes between us. Lying there with her I also caught a glimpse of another place, further than the woodland: great violet hills, where the earth was saffron and the fields were scarlet with poppies. Lakes too, flat surfaces of cobalt. In this land the air was so lucid I saw leaves shivering on trees, worms thrust into the beaks of birds; I saw a bee lost inside the head of a giant buttercup. I saw myself turning away from the nest of Jane and Bill, heading towards those hills, a long road, solemn, a path I would take alone.

Hard sharp bleats pierced this reverie. I glared at the phone. Incredulous, half-conscious. Jane? Just the idea brought on a fit of panic. The phone rang again and again and eventually I rose and walked towards it. I hovered over the phone. But I couldn't pick it up. I felt revulsion then, for Jane and for what she and I had been.

I had already forgotten my wife. It seemed a long time ago. Then Jane's voice came, sad and sober.

"Bill, Bill, it's me."

"Can we meet?"

She sounded lost. She wanted to talk about Lilah, meet in the same pub where we'd met her the night before. Tears fell in straight lines down my cheeks. She was trying to claim me back, claim it all back. Our old life together. Our cold unfucked bed; that's what Lilah had called it. It was all there for the taking, if I wished. I could go back to Jane. Throw Lilah out. Go back to nights sleeping next to Jane, unwanted. Our chaste, childlike pecks on the lips. My cock cowed and penitent. My poor unused cock. How I loved Jane. How I loved her face and her presence in my life; how I loved her and ached for her. And how I needed to reject this chaste fuckless life.

"Bill, I'll be at the pub . . ."

Jane's voice disappeared.

I went back to Lilah who was sprawled on the floor. The kitchen was a mess, like a hurricane had been through. No sign of Choo Choo, no sign of my old life left. My home looked and smelled entirely different. Like a lair, like a cave full of old bones. Like an entirely different couple lived there in my house. Lilah beckoned me to her, and I went. I was pliant and comfortable and still woozy from wine. I can remember Lilah clearly then: her sharp milk teeth – yes. Her green eyes gone murky; now they were rat-brown. Her ears were rodent-like, antennae. I remember how lithe she was, how ferocious her desire to fuck. Lilah licked me over, slavering. On and on she fucked and sucked every drop of me. I knew then, that I was just entertainment. I'd never encountered a creature like her and yet she had humped hundreds like me. I knew I was nothing special, just a dumb man, full of sexual disappointment. Run o' the mill, over-domesticated. I was the average middle-aged bloke; I loved my wife but needed much more sex than I could get. I was your Average Joe, or Bill, for that matter; no one to write home about. She was using me for her amusement, maybe even for a bet? And yet, I didn't care, by then, who or what she was. Only that I was living.

In the hall. On the stairs, on every bed, on the floor, Lilah led me round a merry fuck-happy dance. She was generous, possessing an energy spun up from trees and rivers. I was impregnated with her lust. Lilah sang and smiled and chattered to herself as she fucked. I saw her then, a faerie-sprite. Gay and feckless and wicked. She was charging me up. Jump starting me again; this sex was enlivening, heating my cold loins. Oh, she was generous, oh so generous, licking and fucking and giving me all of herself. Sometimes, she disappeared entirely from sight. I closed my eyes and opened them again to see no one there. Yet I could hear her laugh, giddy with her tricks. I was dazzled by Lilah's light, the gold in her eyes. Her cream skin, her tongue like that of a lily, a deep crimson. Lilah fucked me into an altered state. In those hours I fell in love with her.

*

Lilah left me washed up, exhausted on our marital bed, where I'd slept so carefully with Jane. I fell asleep.

I dreamt of eggs. Fat oval globes. I dreamt that I was trapped inside an egg, my limbs folded like a foetus. It was dark and cool in there, a universe all of my own. The world beyond beckoned with a dim yellow light. But I was comfortable there, it was a place to meditate, safe from Lilah and Jane. I was growing wings inside the egg. I was growing whiskers too, my beard pushing through the follicles on my chin. It was peaceful inside, a place where I overheard echoed conversations from my youth. I travelled back through decades, my twenties and thirties. In the egg, I collected all the time I'd existed. I turned circles inside the egg, upside down, floating in an amniotic fluid. My arms were folded across my chest. I was hanging, suspended. I had another chance to live. I could choose to do things differently. I would gather all I'd been, store it wisely: I could learn from me. I decided then, that I would be a better self in the future. I would hatch, blinking into the sun.

5.

THE SECOND MEETING

JANE

I took the day's issue of The Guardian to use as a prop. I was nervous, but determined not to drink. I sipped mineral water instead, my body buzzing with nerves. I couldn't wait to see Bill, do anything, say everything to make it all right again. I missed him. It felt like we hadn't been in contact for *days*. I was early, so busied myself with the crossword. Usually I'm good at word puzzles, but my head was clogged. Already I was deciding on a trip to a lingerie shop off Upper Street, for a negligee. Or some silk panties. Bill would like silk panties, wouldn't he? I realised then, with horror, how much of Bill I'd ignored. I had to start from scratch.

I'd never sucked my husband's cock. I'd never wanted to. I had performed fellatio many times with other men, but not with Bill. I was consumed with shame and regret. I scribbled words into boxes. So I didn't see Lilah enter the pub. I looked up and there she was, three feet away, on the other side of the table, wearing the same crimson plunging blouse and stonewash jacket and denim skirt from the night before. She'd recently had a bath, I could tell. She was glowing and moist, her short red hair still damp and slicked back. She reeked of bathroom smells, deodorant, shampoo. *My* shampoo, my rose body lotion. She stood with her feet planted wide, her breasts thrust forward, this midget, this bumpkin from Alabama, this whore of the woods, this pixie, imp . . . whatever the fuck she was.

Lilah's face was set in a derisory smile.

"Bill couldn't come," she said.

I stared, as though staring would make me understand. Was Lilah still in our home at lunchtime, when I rang? Had she used our bath? Our towels? Had Bill let her? Had they . . . bathed together? Had he heard my message at all?

"What *the fuck* are you talking about? Where's my husband?"

Slowly, I stood up, towering above her.

"You know. You rang, wanted to talk. About me. Bill didn't want to come to the phone. He can't bring himself to," and her eyes flickered. "Tell you."

I snorted. She was demented. I saw it very clearly then. I had tempted her in. I hadn't guessed what she was. I didn't even know *then* as she stood in front of me, what she was. I'm not sure I even cared. I wondered if there was a way to do this quietly. Offer her money. Threaten her with the police. I could get a restraining order on her. She was delusional. But Lilah, I could see, was following my thoughts. She radiated such strong sexual energy I thought her clothes would burn off.

She scratched at her crotch. Then she sniffed her fingers.

"You disgust me," I said.

"Bill, your dear beloved chaste husband has had a change of . . . heart. You see, you cold cow, something 'unexpected has happened' . . . between me and Bill. I came to tell you. Not to even try coming back."

I laughed. Her tone was superior, her shortness a joke. Her American drawl was highly irritating, antiquated, as if she were reciting it from a language textbook. And the way she kept referring to my husband by his Christian name was inappropriate.

"Where is Bill?"

"At the house."

"Our home?"

"Bill's house," Lilah corrected.

"*Look!* You fucking weird dwarf. You're ridiculous. Do you have any idea *what you're saying*? Do you really expect me to listen to any of this?" I lunged, slapping her hard across the face.

Lilah staggered backwards, clutching her cheek.

I grabbed her by the lapels of her denim jacket. "Listen, I don't know who you are or how you ever got to know me and Bill. I saw you fucking him, okay? I know you think I let you have him. And maybe I did. Maybe I have a part in this. But listen to me and listen good. There is no 'thing' between you and Bill. Do you understand?"

The bar was more or less empty, music playing, the barman on the other side of the bar. But I didn't care if the landlord came over to intervene.

Lilah wasn't the least bit disturbed. Her face was placid. Even though she had a lithe muscular body, she was pliant, yielding. No fight from her then. She smiled at me, pityingly.

"Oh, so now you want him back? Is that right? Bill is a man, not a toy. Now I don't want him, now I do. Is that your kink?"

"Yes." I shouted. "*Yes*, I'm fucked up." I slapped her again, this time twice as hard. Then I held on to her shoulders, almost lifting her from the floor.

She didn't react. "You're the pervert," she said. "The emotional pervert. Twisted as fuck."

"I love my husband," I said. I meant it, but the words fell emptily. I wanted to weep. Now this creature was beating me at my own game, winning over me. I hadn't seen any of it coming.

"What lesson are you trying to teach me?" I said.

"You don't know your husband as well as you think," Lilah whispered and I saw a flicker of her, eyes dilated, glistening, her pearl skin fading to a darker mossy hue. Lumps forming underneath.

"What are you?"

"I have many names. I have whispered them to you. And you ignored them. Never mind."

Lilah grinned and she was beautiful again. Peaches and cream. I loved her then, wanted her too and she knew it. The urge to fuck her came strong and then I was shaking and she laughed at me.

"Happy now? You sad fuck? Happy Miss Cold Fuck who uses her husband, Miss Queen of the Unfucked House? You've never even looked at Bill," she hissed. "You and he are no freakin' match. What we have is ancient, natural. We've been fucking all day, fucked in every room of your cold unfucked home, on the stairs, on your bed. Hours of bliss. He is amazed and doesn't know what to say to you."

I was paralysed. I still held her by the shoulders. Her eyes were alight.

"Whore," I whispered.

She smiled thinly, putting her face up close to mine, sniffed my throat, sniffed my neck, behind my ears, licked me slowly from earlobe to collarbone.

I shuddered.

"Wouldn't you like to fuck me too?" she hissed.

Her hand slid to my pussy. It was wet. Neither of us cared who might be watching. My cheeks reddened. I let her stroke me. I wanted to see what this creature could do. And so I let her stroke me up and down, and it was good. I hated her. And I too could so easily get lost. I was some kind of a virgin.

"Yes, my lonely-for-a-fuck friend. I knew you'd like me too. I am lovely," she pulled opened her blouse enough to reveal one cream breast, a rosy nipple. My own breasts bristled.

I wanted to suckle her.

Lilah smiled.

I was miserable.

Lilah put her hand to her breast and caressed herself.

"No," I tried to blink her from my sight. "Go away." I shoved her away from me.

But there was no way to make Lilah vanish. What she was saying about Bill was ludicrous. She was sinister, worse than I'd imagined, evil. Lying. Cheating. My pussy throbbed. I wanted her. I shook. I began to truly fear her, fear for Bill too. Was she making it all up? I began to see Bill might be in danger. What had she really done with him all day? I saw Bill tied up, or worse. Lilah's eyes flitted over my face, as though reading my thoughts again.

"You think a lot of yourself, don't you Miss Castration?" she rasped. "Always in control, always the onlooker, the thinker. All those clever ideas. I know what you thought of me, you patronising bitch. But you sized me up all wrong. I think you're conceited."

She pulled her blouse closed, buttoning it up. I was sorry to lose the sight of her breasts, sorry and lost. I was barely conscious of her straightening out her skirt, walking away. Tears blurred my eyes. I don't know how long I stayed in that non-descript pub, perhaps some time. Her last words had cut. Was she right? Was she telling the truth? Could Bill have fallen in love with her – over the course of one night? Her words . . . *ancient, natural . . .*

*

The third egg was a spangly sequined box. I found it in a shop in Spitalfields market run by two gay men. Pink and turquoise and yellow, it was Liberace-esque. Bill kept his cufflinks in it. Three years of marriage counted out: three happy years. 'Early days', other couples said to us. I smiled, a little nervous, wanting to know more, like what constituted a proper marriage? Twenty, thirty years? *Early days*, it sounded ominous: were later days not as good, less fun, more arduous? I became a couple-watcher, often watching couples who'd been together a long time. How happy were they in their tasteful homes with their tasteful children, what deal had these couples struck? When had the sex vanished, when did these couples stop loving each other that way? When did fatigue set in? Spiritual, emotional death? Were any of those couples hiding what I was?

Soon after I gave Bill the third egg, a flurry of dreams hatched. The egg triggered the dreams, I have no doubt about that. The third egg started it all. The dreams came creamy, phantom-like, slipping like smoke out from beneath a door. I dreamt of other men, mornings, mostly. I woke up entwined with someone I'd met in real life: men from all kinds of chance encounters, men I'd only met once or twice, work acquaintances, other women's husbands. Men who'd passed me on the road, one in a white van, another in a silver Jag. Or men who I'd known in the past who I'd ignored or turned down. Likewise, men I'd yearned for and who'd never wanted me: they all returned in my dreams.

Waking up in bed next to Bill, having made love to another man, brought excruciating pangs of guilt. As if my adultery had been real, as if my dream trysts were alive and illicit, somehow actual and fulfilled. They were passionate, uncomplicated, always benevolent. And insistent: I couldn't stop them. The dreams happened of their own accord, tumbling out on the backs of other dreams. I would wake in another man's arms, my husband inches from me, his body big and warm. Or I would be lying on my back on the same bed, tempting another man to me with my long legs.

I enjoyed numerous trysts, the men becoming strangers, eccentric, exotic playboys. In one dream I met a man in a coffee shop round the corner from our home, a place I frequented: he was blond, American, a fire tattoo raging on the inside of his forearm. A clown, he said, by profession, set himself alight while wearing a straightjacket on stage. He was on edge, his face was angular. I imagined leather and pain and something else in his eyes. This man was feral, somehow, from lack of love, from his sad clown's job. Where had he emerged from, how had I conjured him up? We ate peach melba from a bowl with two spoons. He had large blue goldfish eyes. When he kissed me across the table I was caught by surprise. *Be my lover,* he whispered. Outside, we kissed in the street, his lips like butterflies on my neck. The spokes of his bike were pretty, sprinkled with butterflies.

Another of my dream-men was a scientist. We went to a cheap hotel in South Kensington. I was sipping a glass of red wine at the window, looking out on to London rooftops. He came on me from behind, shed all my clothes very quickly, peeling off my bra. *Gorgeous* – he gasped, my breasts were exposed to the skies. We sank to the small single bed. We fucked and fucked. Later we ordered room service, ate smoked salmon sandwiches and fruit salad. The night porter rang: *is your guest staying the night?* Yes, my dream-lover slammed the phone down. His bed-manners were impeccable, though. Once he stopped to wipe cum from my stomach with a clean towel. His cock was slender, ladylike. *I fall in love with every woman I sleep with*, he said. We fucked some more and I covered his chest and biceps in tiny rosy-red bites.

The dreams were oh-so-satisfying. Like watching a wordless play, one in which I never knew who would step out of the shadows of the wings. Countless animus projections: older men, younger men. Men who knew me. Fathers, sons, married men. Clowns, scientists, poets. I was never in control. I was slowed down, though, often on rerun. But never thoughtful or conscious of myself at all. I came to understand the dreams were some kind of call – away from Bill? Was it a part of me trying to find itself? Yes. A part of me, against my will, was bidding to be activated.

Then the dreams came thick and fast, every morning, in the bath, during the day too, a hundred men come to take me away. Liberate me, smash up my marriage. We were no match – exactly as Lilah had said, exactly her words. The urge to leave Bill was ever-present, a secret I pondered every day then tucked away – until the next dream. The dreams were powerful and persistent – premonitions? The truth: I was wretched by the time we met Lilah in that bar.

I hardly turned to Bill for sex. While my immense love had grown, my interest in him, physically, ebbed away. Even though I liked the look of Bill, even though I liked his sandalwood scent, even though I liked the way he moved. Even though I wasn't repulsed at all – I wasn't moved. I wasn't pestered to fuck him, not like the men in the dreams, oh those wretched dreams. I looked to Bill for other things. I felt guilt, but also innately knew my dreams were good for me, they were pictures, snapshots of possibility. Isn't that the job of fantasy? To envision one's potential? They were flashes of a future I wanted. I looked around and half-guessed, half-hoped, the same conflict lurked in other women's lives.

Intuitively, Bill didn't press. He seemed content enough to be with me, he often came to bed later and by then I was asleep. Or else we would read for an hour or so, using the book as a prop, me reading next to him too. How many books did we use as bed dividers? Sex became something we didn't mention let alone do. God knows what he was really thinking; God knows how he coped. He loved me, or so I thought up until the day we met Lilah in that bar. I thought Bill loved me so much he wanted us to keep going any way. I thought I wanted this too.

Secretly, I wondered just how long this could go on: months, a year had gone past. Many years? *Early days . . .* is this what other older, wiser, more successful couples meant? That there would be hardships, like this? Was I to look forward to years, a decade of making do, avoiding the subject? I was still young. So was Bill. It wasn't right.

Then, Lilah showed up. My crime wasn't to underestimate Lilah, but to underestimate my own desires. Without spending this desire, a well had built up. A store of energy which demanded release. I went inward and got mixed up. By the time Lilah appeared, I had lost my judgement, nourished myself for too long from dreams. I simply dreamt up another scene.

After Lilah left the bar I ordered a stiff drink, a double gin, then two more. I got drunk. I liked to drink. Had an imp hexed my family once, centuries back? It was our thing, to drown in a bottle. It made everything slow and soft and better. I decided I would go to our home. I imagined Lilah had returned there, but God knows what she'd said to Bill, if anything. Had she even cut the phone line? Tampered with it? Had she blocked the call I'd made? Anything could be possible. I would go home, confront Bill, forbid whatever was going on between my husband and this slut. Her news was absurd. According to Lilah, over one night, Bill had fallen in love with her.

Forgotten our years together. He had thrown everything away for one great fuck. Could he? Had things been that bad, for him? What wickedness had this Lilah-creature been up to? I thought of her hand on my pussy, the searing pleasure. What, in my absence, had she done to Bill? I wept. I was scared, unsure of myself. I ordered another gin. Something I'd read . . . came to me. Iron. From the few facts I'd picked up on the dark web I'd read these creatures were allergic to iron. Iron could damage them, even prove fatal. It was a useful piece of information. My drink arrived. The barman acted as though he hadn't seen Lilah come and go. Was she invisible to others? By then, I was hammered. I wanted my home back, my life as it was. I wanted to speak to my husband.

LILAH

I scared Miss Sexual Desert good and proper, but found myself quite shaken too. In the cab on the way back I touched my cheek where she'd slapped me twice. The sting was still there, surprising. Heat in her after all, the little prig. I don't think she believed what I said about me and Bill; I could hardly believe what I'd said myself, that I was journeying back to Bill, paying a cab to take me to him. *Something has happened between me and Bill.* What had been happening to me? Being outdoors in the fresh air had given me a taste of reality again. Whatever had been going on in that creepy house between us had to stop. It was only twenty-four hours since I'd met this dreary couple in a bar, a pair like so many others – Jane and Bill, Janet and Joe, Mary and Pete, just like many I'd encountered. Same deal.

And yet this time it had been different. I hadn't escaped so easily. I'd prevaricated because of this new feeling. I hastily took stock. I had stayed on a hunt long after the kill. I had met a lover in the form of a man in the human realm. A First. Bill could meet me, match my skills. Bill had located my spot, caused me to gush like no other, not even Samael. And – was there more? There had been another aspect which I found hard to name, a feeling which had swiftly passed over me during our hours of sexing. It had been a flash of a rich, full feeling. I had felt an empathy with Bill, like he was more than just a mortal man. Bill had stirred me up and I wasn't accustomed to this chaotic mixture of feelings inside.

Whatever these new 'feelings' were or had been, they had disappeared. Vamoosed. I couldn't remember them. Love? Ha. I felt like my old self again. I felt itchy. Loose. I wanted to be on my way, back into the forest. I remembered the cat, Choo Choo. I thought of the hexacious tower I'd created, amidst all that iron. I had stamped my mark on this couple, I always do. I had reconfigured things between them, and that was what the wife had wanted me to do. Too bad if she had changed her mind. Too bad. And Bill, well, he had given me a turn. I had taken my life in my hands to have intercourse with him. He was one to remember. Okay, I said to myself: there's nothing like experience. This man Bill has been a first. I will go and say goodbye to him.

Bill greeted me at the door with decisive amorous kisses. I'd only been gone a couple of hours, but already he wanted more of my talents; he was tugging at my clothes, trying to remove my skirt. I pushed him off. That constant shocked expression had disappeared. He looked different. Pinker in the cheeks. He wanted more of me and I'd had enough of him.

"Thank God you're back. I fell asleep, didn't find your note at first. I . . . panicked."

"I went to see your wife."

"*What*?"

"Yeah. I wish I hadn't."

"I wish you hadn't either. What did she say?"

"What do you *think* she said? The usual jealous wife stuff. Do you care?"

A strange look came into his eyes. Soft. Thoughtful.

"I don't want you to disappear like that again."

I stared at him.

"What are you saying?"

Bill wanted to keep me there. He'd struck gold and fuck, shit, damn and hell – yes, he was expecting I might even like to stay with him!

"Me? Stay here with you in this creepy old house, with all these red and yellow walls – me? You freakin kidding me?"

"We can paint them white – or black – or whatever you want. Just stay, another night, at least. Stay a week. A month. However long you like. I was . . . worried."

"Why should I stay?"

"For the same reason other imps like you have stayed with men. To be happy. Wouldn't you like it here? What's your home like? A hut? A bender made of twigs? An earth-floored cave in the woods? Do you live underground? Eh? What? Surely this must have some appeal?"

"Get lost," I snarled.

"Always so mean, eh? Is that it? I'm to be chewed up and spat out, is that right?"

"Go fuck yourself."

"And where's my cat, eh? Choo Choo. Where is he? Scared him off too?"

"Oh, fuck your cat."

"Have you fucked my cat?" He said this with a knowing smirk.

I threw myself at Bill, tore at him and wreaked my vengeance and distaste on him and their Goddamn marriage. I turned nasty on him, biting him and this time when we were fucking we were like cats fighting. Furniture tumbled around us. Again, I was matched.

Bill pinned me down and then he fucked me senseless and dear-God-in-heaven more than anything – this was not okay. This was why I fled in the first place, to be so taken like this by the very first man ever made. Rape. It was all women were to expect. And so my foremother Lilith ran and ran away from man and God, only to be further humiliated in the desert. She was so angry then, she made daemons, thousands of them every day, her offspring. She became an outcast, forever. I spat at Bill and fought, but he held me down and then he fucked me hard and rough and a pearly liquid gushed from between my legs, a silken waterfall slipping out. My whole body spasmed in the fullness of my orgasm. He could make me come just like that. It was as if he'd learnt the knack. And all the while I thought: *I am lost, lost. Go home, get out of here.* I was embarrassed, torn open. I hated him then. I didn't want to look Bill in the eye. He thought he now had some power over me because he could make me gush. When he was done he withdrew, his own body shuddering, his semen still dripping. His cock hadn't shrivelled with the release, it still looked plump and even ready for more. Bill glowed, exulted with his conquest. I'm sure he thought he'd turned a trick himself. He kissed my stomach. But I was cold to him, cold in my heart.

The atmosphere had changed between us. I was desperate to flee. I suggested I cook him a meal, the only meal I can prepare, French toast. Bill was happy with this; he went out to potter in his workshop. I tied on one of her aprons and cracked eggs into a bowl, turning the radio on. I was determined to vanish as soon as possible. I'd make him a Goddamn wife-meal, except I'd sprinkle in some narcotic herbs; yeah, I'd drug Bill up, leave while he slept. Everything had got to me, especially their nest. All their photos and knick-knacks. It made my skin crawl, all the trappings of a so-called happy home. I became moody and morbid. I suffered some kind of attack, a whirling in my head, a fluttering in my heart. My cunt still pulsed with the after-pleasure of a good hard fuck. The urge to return to the woodland was overwhelming.

BILL

When I awoke, Lilah was gone. Panic seized me and immediately I was up and alert and searching the house, then outside in the garden and then my workshop, fearful she'd left for good. Miserable, I was more frightened of losing Lilah than Jane. Lilah was who I'd imagined since boyhood, Lilah was stepped out of the shadows of my closeted dreams. I had found her, *anima perfecta*, anima extraordinaire. And then she'd vanished.

Then – thank God. I came across a note on the kitchen table, a fine calligraphy in turquoise ink – explaining she had gone to the pub to meet Jane. I made strong black coffee and gazed at the kitchen strewn with the aftermath of Lilah's visit. Flies buzzed over the honeyed crumbs and the beetroot ink had now left permanent stains on the floor. It was late Monday afternoon. I tried to recover time, count the hours since Jane and I went to the pub the night before with Sebastian. Not even twenty-four hours had passed. A malevolent odour hung in the air, neither fruit nor meat, something dank and indefinable. A pile of soft purple fruit, like plums, had appeared in the hallway; what were they?

The living room was as we'd left it the night before, my clothes and Lilah's over the floor, furniture. Vinyl records pulled from their sleeves, our mugs and cups and open shopping bags left haphazard. A whirlwind had passed through. And still no sign of Choo Choo.

I went outside and called his name. I clanged his metal dish with a fork. Choo Choo was a good judge. I wanted him to meet Lilah, for them to clap eyes on each other.

I wanted to gauge Choo Choo's reaction to her. I called and put some tuna in his bowl. When he didn't appear, I worried. I drank the coffee on a wooden kitchen chair out in the sun. Over the garden wall my neighbour started up his lawn mower, an air-cutting growl. The sun beat down. *Oh, Jane, what were you thinking? Now I am lost. Is that what you wanted?* The thought of Lilah brought on an ache in the gut, the thighs. The thought of Jane made me feel safe in the world. But right then I was alone. I had lost both women.

The sun beat down. A giant yolk in the sky.
  I will live differently.
  I waited for inspiration, to know what to do. My eyes swam, droplets emerged on my forehead.
  A fly landed on my bare belly, walking down to my navel as if towards a cave. It was all I could do not to slip off the chair. I wanted to shout for help, over the fence, at my neighbour. My cry would be drowned by the mower.
  I wanted to live a new way.
  The sky was an immense field of blue. Nothing in it. The words for prayers eluded me.
  Where was Choo Choo?

When Lilah returned I was beside myself. I wanted to know what Jane had said, what Lilah had said in reply. I was shocked to hear Jane had slapped Lilah, twice, threatened her; I was amazed and concerned that this confrontation had happened. I prodded Lilah for more information. But she was distracted and unforthcoming, no longer interested in the story. Not much more to report, she said. She had seen Jane off.

"Why did you ever like her?" Lilah spat.

"I loved her."

"She's a patronising cunt. How much longer were you going to live with her all celibate like that? Years?"

"I loved her."

"She took care of you. But what about the flesh? Were you waiting till you dick shrivelled off?"

"Yes."

"What kind of love is that?"

"The love that comes down from the heavens, from God."

"*Love.* That's all you humans talk about. She never loved you. She's as twisted as an old tree stump."

"No. I always understood her. I knew what kind of love she was talking about. I knew. I don't think I ever told her that I understood. I resented her too much, but I understood."

"Her *holy* love of you."

"Yes."

"Ugh. Jane and her holy love, the Saviour of Men's Hearts and Banisher of Men's Hard-Ons. For fuck's sake. She's a sanctimonious holy cunt."

"I loved her."

"You poor fuck. She wanted to leave you, run off. That's why she invited me here."

"I know."

"What do you mean you *know*?"

"You think I didn't twig what you women were up to? You think I'm that dumb?"

"Most men are."

Lilah's eyes turned cold. For the first time she became aloof, sizing me up. I was scared of her then, the hairs on the back of my neck and arms stood up. Her eyes fired. She threw herself at me and then she was on me, fighting and biting me with all her wrath, as if to kill me off. I saw the horror of her then, a small beast, covered in coarse brown hair. I tried to protect myself, ward her off, but she fought me harder, and I was scared, but also turned on. Lilah, in her fury, had released an odour, some thick heady musk which brought on a ferocious ardour. My cock became hard as rock, I wanted to fuck her and yet she was fighting me, trying her best to harm me. We fell and collapsed on the floor, around us chairs clattered and then I had her pinned down, snarling at me, fangs bared.

Everything she said over the last twenty-four hours rang in my ears. I was inside her quickly, leaving my senses behind. I saw her as my bride, my eternal partner, sensed an infinite oneness as we fucked and writhed. I was putting myself back together, in her. Lilah screamed and beat me with her fists. But I couldn't let up my outpouring of grief for the man I wanted to be and hadn't yet been, for the love I had always wanted and had only ever tasted here, with this fickle creature. *I will live differently, I will live differently.* Waves and waves of agony, all those years without sleep, without sex, without this union with another being. I fucked and fucked Lilah and lost myself and saw Lilah too was in agony, shouting, begging me to stop. She was crying with terror. I was raping her, and I didn't know how to stop myself. I was in some kind of trap with her. A liquid gushed from her legs, like albumen. Hot and silken to touch. I felt elated at this release, hoping something inside her had melted, that this fluid was proof she had melted. But I was wrong. Lilah wasn't human. When I looked down into Lilah's eyes, they were cold. Hateful.

6.
IRON

JANE

I collected myself and left the pub, hailing a black cab. Sitting in the back, I suddenly thought about Choo Choo. I hadn't seen him earlier that morning either; where had he gone? And when he returned, just how had Lilah treated him? Or he treated Lilah? I hoped he had peed in her handbag. I had a friend in Choo Choo. I hoped he was, at the very least, inhospitable. There were things about my married life which would surely put Lilah in her place: framed photographs of us, our books, our homely house, our neighbours. Lilah was a stranger, a one-night stand. No match for our relationship.

I saw the route I'd take. I wouldn't be cold, aloof with Bill. I wouldn't be grief-stricken either, pathetic. I wouldn't beg or cry. None of that. No cringing or falling to pieces, no blame either. I didn't want to confess what I'd done to Bill and I didn't want Bill's explanations. I didn't want him to feel guilty, either. I had put this affair into action. Now it was up to me to deactivate the plan. Pull them apart, if need be. I would fight, physically, for my husband and my home. I would scratch her eyes out, rip off those pointy ears. I knew iron could damage her badly if need be. I had some ideas.

Our house came into view. My stomach lurched. I paid the driver with stiff fingers, not bothering to collect the change. The front door was closed. I couldn't believe she was still there; I hadn't invited her *to stay*. I fumbled in my bag for my door keys as I strode up the garden path. My hands shook as I turned the key and opened the front door. There was music on, and I sensed someone up ahead, in the kitchen. To the right, the living room was a shock. Cups, mugs everywhere, piles of ash, cigarette butts, empty bottles of wine, dirty plates. Bill's shirt hung over an arm of the sofa. Bill's old vinyl records lay strewn about, pulled from their sleeves. A dank and heavy odour I couldn't identify hung in the air, unpleasant, earthy: rotting meat? On the floor, in the middle of the hallway, there was a pyramid. A pile of what looked like dried fruit, figs or maybe plums.

I stood in the centre of the sitting room, awed. I wanted to scream. No one had heard me enter the house. Here was what I'd left behind. Lilah's handbag was still on the sofa. And then – I seemed to know of her theft. I scanned the bookshelves for the eggs I'd given Bill, my eggs. They'd vanished.

"B . . . Bill?" I stammered, my eyes wet.

Slowly, I walked down the hall, avoiding the fruit. Music was playing in the kitchen, The Neville Brothers on the radio. I stood for several moments, unobserved. The kitchen looked like another place. It had been ruined. Purple ink stains all over the floor, and the vegetable box had been upended and left, vegetables all over the place and bags of shopping scattered and empty bottles of wine and champagne and open milk and juice cartons and flies buzzing, the sink crammed with dishes and the stink of rotting food in the humid heat of the early evening. The place looked crazy, as if teenagers had been having a party.

I gaped.

Lilah was there, at the stove, wearing one of my aprons, her back to me. She stood at the cooker, frying something. She was barefoot, humming along to the tune. I tried to speak.

Bill appeared at the open French window. He looked at me and nodded stiffly, with only faint recognition. He went over to the radio and turned down the music, as if he was about to do that anyway. Then he turned to look at me, but couldn't quite meet my eyes.

"Hi," he said quietly, shiftily.

By then Lilah had seen me too, but kept herself busy at the cooker. She was sawing, cutting up something, bread? I stared at Bill. He was dishevelled, tired.

"Look at me, Bill." I said.

He looked into my face, but his manner was detached.

"Bill. What is Lilah still doing here?"

Bill ran his hands though his hair. He groaned, expelling a pent-up and long-held patience. He began to pace.

"Bill, I want her to go. Do you hear me? Whatever has happened between you, we need to talk. I think we . . ."

Bill stopped. "Look, Jane, I . . . think you should apologise."

I stared.

"*Me?* Apologise . . . for what? For *what* Bill," my voice was barely audible.

"For insulting Lilah earlier. For what you said to her in the pub, for trying to scare her. You slapped her, didn't you? I think you should say sorry." Bill looked at Lilah.

Lilah turned and smiled thinly.

"Bill!" I shouted. "I am *your wife*. Remember? What has happened to you? Bill?"

Bill didn't respond. He shrugged, this wasn't something he wanted to discuss. This Bill was a different man. This Bill was awkward, cool. He minded my presence;

clearly it bothered him to have me there. I'd intruded on something. Lilah was sawing a loaf of bread, both of them were detached – as if I wasn't even visible. She dipped the slices of bread into a bowl of runny egg mixture. She was making French toast for Godssake.

I screamed. "*Bill.*" I stamped my foot. "What the fuck is going on?"

Bill looked at me, baleful, serious for the first time. "I thought Lilah had tried to explain . . . "

"Explain *what*, Bill? I want YOU to explain. Tell me what she said. Tell me what . . . go on."

Bill had a pitying expression in his eyes. "I'm sorry," was all he could say.

"Sorry?"

Bill paced.

"Sorry? For what?"

Lilah turned round. Her face was steely, pensive. I picked up the nearest heavy object to hand, a book resting on the countertop, an old recipe book, and hurled it.

It hit the wall, *thwack*.

Lilah's placid face broke, her eyes fired.

"You creepy fucking bitch. Get out of my house." I picked up a large glass ashtray – and hurled that too. *Smack*. Closer this time, I was trying to cause a scene, drama, anything to break the spell between them. But neither of them flinched. Lilah continued to fry her soggy bread. Bill just stood there.

Then, I snapped.

I hurled anything and everything I could: a bowl, *thwack*. More books, I pelted apples from the bowl, bananas, oranges. One of Bill's shoes. My missiles banged, thumped and exploded, knocking over other objects, ricocheting off cupboards, walls. Lilah put her hands up to shield herself.

"Take this, you fucking witch," I was wild but I hadn't even started yet. I would kill her, kill her off. That vixen was no match; I would send her home.

"Out, *witch!*" I shouted. "Begone. This is my house. Begone, you devil-whore."

I pulled a picture off the wall and hurled that, the glass smashing against the kitchen taps. "Out! Out with you. Whoever you are."

I was shouting, hysterical, telling her to go, leave, fuck off, get out of my home, to leave immediately. I had gathered my own power then. The kettle stood near me and I ripped out its lead. I began to swing it like a whip, whacking the countertops. Lilah was frozen, her eyes on me. I swung the lead in a frenzy, my veins rushing.

I shouted at Bill.

"Can't you *see*? Can't you see what she is? Look at her fucking ears, she's a freak, she's not right, not human, Bill can't you see? Bill, Bill, look at her ears!" I bellowed. "Get out, whore. Pest. Out of my house." Then Bill was behind me, his heavy hands clamping down on my arms. I turned and elbowed him hard in the throat. He recoiled, choking. Lilah had grabbed the lead and we were playing tug-o'-war, her pointy teeth bared. Her eyes were black and leaden.

Lilah growled, like a cornered dog. I let go of the lead and she stumbled backwards.

A heavy iron-bottomed frying pan hung from a hook by the wall. I knew then I would do it. I grabbed it by the handle. Lilah shrieked as though I were brandishing a club of fire. Her eyes rolled backwards and she began to plead.

"Not *that*. Please not that. I'll do anything, please, no. I'll go, I'll go. I was just about to leave."

Lilah wailed, the sound cutting into my bones. On and on, but it only made me feel more powerful, wanting to polish her off. At last, I had the means to get rid of her.

I hit her with the heavy pan – clubbing her again and again until she was on the floor, until she was begging and crying and pleading and protecting her head with her arms, weeping. I beat and beat and beat her, shouting God knows what, "Out, storm; out, strangler; crusher, darkener of the light; out, you bitch-whore." Murder flourished in me, a sheer blind fury. Nothing could stop me. I wasn't leaving. She was the one who was leaving.

"Jane, *stop*."

Bill was on me again. This time he picked me up bodily and pulled me off Lilah. I was still wielding the frying pan and my legs kicked, my body writhed as he hauled me away from her, out of the kitchen, along the hall. I saw the pyramid of fruit again, the soft plump balls. What were they? We left Lilah crumpled on the floor, badly wounded. I was glad. I wanted to kill her.

"Look Bill," I shouted. "What's that? She's some kind of witch. What the fuck is that thing on the floor?" Bill took no notice. "She was making the same pile in the pub. Didn't you see?"

At the bottom of the stairs Bill stopped and turned me to face him. He shackled my hands in his and pressed my back to the wall. We were inches apart, my body heaving, blood boiling. I could have clubbed Bill too, then. Stalked off leaving them both dead.

"Now you listen to me," Bill's voice was calm, and he looked me straight in the eye. "I think we all know why Lilah's here. I know about your little game, okay? That you *wanted* her to be here. I know how you feel . . . about me. I know about your dreams, your dream-men. Sometimes you talk in your sleep, Jane. Sometimes you tell me all about these other men. And you know what . . . you should take this opportunity to leave. Wasn't that your idea?"

I began to sob, shake. "I'm so sorry," I stuttered, unable to look at him. "I didn't mean any of this. I was happy, Bill. I just . . . well. I didn't know how to talk about it. What to say. Last night I was drunk. I was stupid, an idiot. I didn't mean this to happen. Not this. I want to *stay*. Please. Bill, I love you. Can we talk, please. Bill, please?"

Bill's expression turned distant.

Lilah had risen from the floor. She was standing behind us. Her presence cooled the room. She was severely bruised by my assault. Blue-black marks had already bloomed on her face, around her eyes, cheekbones; the marks were spreading as I watched. Her head looked tipped a little to one side. One ear looked mangled. I had clubbed that side of her head. She cradled a glass of milk in her hands. They could call the police if they wanted to, have me arrested. I hated her. I'd never encountered such a pest. She gulped her milk like a child, leaving a moustache.

"I'll pack a suitcase," I stuttered. "Give me ten minutes."

*

In our bedroom, I pulled a suitcase from above the wardrobe. I snatched as many clothes as I could off the rails and threw them in. Jeans, jackets, cardigans. I opened my dresser draws, flinging anything and everything into it, all my underwear, jumpers, T-shirts. I found another case and filled it with shoes. I was terrified. Terrified of Lilah. What had she done to Bill? How had she caused this radical change in him? I wanted to go. I would go to the police. Tell them about Lilah: about what had happened to us. Maybe they already knew about her. She was dangerous, a danger to others. My hands trembled. That lugubrious odour again, it stunned my nostrils. It was stronger here than on the ground floor. A sweet, hot, cloying stench in the air. Something was up here; something was dead. I hurried to the bathroom for my spongebag and toothbrush.

In the mirror – I saw myself. Eyes ringed with red, a cut on my top lip. On the little shelf under the mirror stood Bill's fat badger hair shaving brush, a present from me. I laughed as he had teased Choo Choo with it, running it past Choo Choo's nose like a mouse.

Choo Choo. The stink was very near, overpowering. It was extremely hot in the bathroom too, a sauna. I turned away from the mirror, stared at the cupboard in the corner – the boiler was in there. Our airing cupboard, it was where we kept the towels and linen. I advanced, cringing. Tears fell; my throat was a hard ball. I pulled open the doors. Piles of neatly folded towels, sheets, and, between some old tablecloths, Choo Choo's stiffened body was stretched out. His eyes were bulged, his tongue hung from his open mouth. He looked outraged, as if he had been fighting until his last breath. He had been throttled, his neck twisted and snapped. This would have taken some strength.

I backed away. Hot tears fell down my face.

"Who is she?" I whispered. What had I let in? A desolate feeling came over me, of love, of my love for Bill now ruined, possibly forever. My one true love. I wanted to kill Lilah off, run downstairs with the iron pan, swinging and roaring. But I knew I would be stopped. Something had indeed happened to Bill. I ran back to the bedroom, knowing my time was running short. I gave the room a final spot check, opening the dresser drawers. In one I found, right at the back, in a corner, a small paper bag. I picked up the bag and rustled open the tissue inside, realising what it was.

The fourth egg I bought for Bill was tiny and beautiful, opals embedded in rock. Polished and buffed, exquisite, caramel and red, veined with lilac crystals and flecks of opaline. Bill's birthday was three weeks away, always just after our anniversary.

Four years. I hid the egg from him, as was my custom. I was dying to give it to him, watch his face light up. I held the small egg in the palm of my hand: it was perfect. Graceful. Omnipotent. The beginning of all things. I propped the egg up on the windowsill, the tissue around it like a nest, leaving it for Bill to discover later.

Then I ran downstairs, hauling my cases. I went to the kitchen to collect my handbag. I saw Lilah sitting there at the kitchen table. Her face was unrecognisable, swollen and misshapen. One eye bulged. A thick clear liquid seemed to be oozing and dripping. Bill was tending to her, but she was groaning. Neither of them seemed to care I was there or see me go. For the second time that day, I let myself out. My home was different now. It was no longer mine. I stepped out into the warm summer evening, the evening after the midsummer solstice. I had got what I wanted after all. I was free to meet all those men, to enjoy all the trysts I'd ever dreamt about.

LILAH

I heard the front door open, her footsteps in the hall. I even heard her awe, the tears choke in her throat. I hated her then and hated them both. I was part of something I no longer wanted to be part of. I had stayed much too long, got confused. I was trapped in their marriage. Had I fallen for Bill? Fallen in the way humans do, foolishly, unwisely, without a thought. If so, I hated myself for it. My head was cluttered with thoughts, too many thoughts: go, stay, run. By the time Jane arrived I'd had enough. I was plotting my escape. I was cursing myself for this mess, this God-awful freakin' mess I was in. Leave, go. Never mind about Bill. I turned my back on Miss Janey-Wife, pretending I couldn't hear her, pretending I was engrossed in making French toast.

"Bill, Bill," she wheedled, pitiful.

My blood chilled river-cold.

"Speak to me. Bill."

But he couldn't.

"Bill, I am your wife. *Bill.*"

Pathetic sobs, Janey-Wife pleaded. She wanted me to go and began to curse me and use her own magic. *Witch*, *whore*, she began with my more common names. Oh, she had gathered herself and this is all a human female needs to do: use her own power against me. Many cower. Some run. Most fall for all the tricks. I have always used the men and then won the women; a good cunt lick will soften a woman up. Few face me.

And Goddamn I wanted to go too. She and I had both had enough. We felt the same way, maybe. Bill was the only one still engaged in this useless tryst. We females had both come to the same conclusion. The game was over. I wanted to climb out the window, disappear right then; that would give them something to talk about. But Bill wouldn't speak to her, couldn't explain himself. *Something has happened*, I wanted to scream, *something bad has happened between us. All your fault, all your doing. Happy now?* She looked incredulous, she, Lady Unfucked, Lady Double Cross My Husband – of all people, wanting explanations. And then, when she couldn't get him back, just like a child, she stamped her foot and began to hurl things at the wall. A little blizzard of shoes, books, fruit. She began to utter cries of *out* – a banishing that can work, and yet her banishments were too weak. She didn't know what she was doing, to banish an imp like me takes more concerted magic. I loved her then, for she showed some of Lilith in her fury, her daemon had come up. We were eye-to-eye, she and me, I loved her then, almost called her sister-whore.

"I love you," I taunted.

And then she picked up an iron pan. I had noticed it earlier and kept clear. She came at me like a true shedim, wanting to kill me off. And well, then everything was lost. She had enough of the devil in her then, her hatred and fear was unleashed, all of it. Years of distilled loneliness and fear, all her untapped lust. It flew out.

*

I cannot remember too much of her attack: or rather I don't like to recall her wrath, for my premonition had been accurate. I'd stayed far too long, stumbled into a complicated set up between a couple who weren't fucking. That freakin' workshop too. Damn it, I had been attracted to Bill, had been bewitched or whatever humans like to call the spell of love.

Now I'm forever damaged by her fury. I look in the mirror sometimes and weep for what I've lost, for what I am now – a hag. My luxurious crown of red hair has fallen in patches, never to re-grow. One eye has turned inward. My jaw is twisted. I have lost my youthful body too. My bones are thinner, my skin is lacklustre. I am diminished in stature, crippled. One of her many blows caught the side of my head. I am deaf.

Now, I will never cross-over again. I will never sit in bars alone, all shiny and new as a glistening cobweb. I will never enjoy the gaze of mortal men, never tempt them away from those who already shun them. I will never lead men astray, use my charms and sex magick to give them what they want. I cannot fathom the kind of love those two shared, a wholesome giving love only meant for children. But I reckon she got what she wanted in the end, that holy cunt of an unhappy wife. I imagine her now, enjoying herself, using her sexiness.

In the end, there was no midnight flit. I was already turning a vivid blue-black and I knew the bruising would get worse. Bill was beside himself.

"Tell me what to do, tell me, please." But I sat him down amongst the wreckage and explained it was all my doing. I was at fault: I'd stayed too long. I needed to go home, back to my people.

I am hideous as well as beautiful and I let my natural face show, the face which is unacceptable in public in the human realm.

"This is what I am," I said, lovingly.

Bill, my love, my one true love. The last man I crossed over to meet and still think of, from time to time, mostly first thing in the mornings. I wake with wet eyes; I ache to think of Bill, my love, I suffer pains in the chest just thinking of what we shared.

Bill shrieked. "Dear *God,* no."

He sobbed and shook at the sight of the grotesque being that I am, the woodlander who lives underground. The First Wife of all men; that she-witch – is my mother. She was the First Model. A mistake. Devilish and insubordinate. I am one of her great-great granddaughters, one who lived, for her offspring were routinely murdered. I scared him, then, good and proper.

I found my handbag and took off Janey-Wife's apron and left quietly by the front door. I was relieved it was all over. I left my hex encrypted in the sculpture I had constructed in Bill's workshop. Not a complicated hex, a smidgen of her fantasies and lies, a bucket full of his yearnings. I mixed them good and spat on them and left the spittle as glue, my contempt for all they chose to hide from each other. Fuck that little prude, Miss Unfucked-Pussy-of-the-Night. Fuck her eggs and her fantasy life; I'm glad I caused her harm, glad of her regrets. They will be eternal. Yes, she will go on to meet many men, to enjoy her pussy and enjoy her sex. Regular little Sex Pot she will become and yet it will cost her something. Regret will be her new pest.

BILL

On my worktable, Lilah's obelisk was a work of some ingenuity. Constructed with skill, an almost architectural expertise in the way all the pieces chosen had fitted so snugly together. Even so, I found it sinister. What it was, I still don't know. Carbuncular, ornate. It was some kind of mosaic, something organic and even alive. At times I saw it actually shifting, ever so minutely, as though its surfaces were juggling to get comfortable. For days I kept away from it, instinctively. I wanted to smash it down, but the tower imposed itself and I didn't dare. I tinkered at another desk, my back to it.

But I couldn't ignore the malevolent feeling it gave out, a shadow passing across my back. *Dear Jane, all this came from you, from your thoughts, your nameless faceless trysts. Well done.*

It was early evening when Jane returned, not long after Lilah. She must have followed Lilah back and I'm still moved she chose this path; that, after all her crimes of fantasy-infidelity, she felt remorse. Jane wanted to fight for our relationship, wanted a battle. It didn't make sense.

I didn't hear Jane enter the house. I wandered over to the patio doors by chance – and there she was. I was unable to open my mouth, shout her down for her betrayal. I barely met her eyes, simply went over in a deranged half-believing state to turn the music down. Lilah remained calm, frying up some bread dipped in egg, her back to Jane. The atmosphere was poisonous. Both women were loaded with malevolent feeling. No one spoke. Like a fish bowl, everything was silent and the space between us was fluid.

Fire blazed in Jane's eyes. Incomprehension in her voice. Enough to melt me. "Bill, Bill," she repeated, "What's going on here?" and me unable to reply, to find the right response. I couldn't extend any sympathy to her at all. Was Jane that perverted after all, just like Lilah had said? She had set me up and now she was enquiring what was wrong. Go fuck yourself, Jane, I should have shouted. I should have bellowed in her face. Maybe it should have been me and Jane who had that fight with the frying pan. "Bill, Bill." Her pathetic pleading voice. "I am your wife." As if to get me back. Jane stamped her foot and began throwing things about, wreaking vengeance, attacking Lilah, hurling books and shoes, fruit, anything she could get her hands on. Lilah, at this point, was still placid.

Which of those women was the witch then? Which was the creature loosed from the mud? I had never seen Jane in such a state, swinging and lashing out. Fighting for her home, happiness, all she had at stake. Cursing and threatening Lilah, calling back her arid queendom. Queen Jane. Queen of the Unfucked Bed. Her hair was loose and her eyes were gleaming and she was more alive than I'd ever seen her. What was she fighting for? Me? Us? A blood lust was up in her. Too late – too late. I had been unfaithful to Jane and yet somehow, also, I was the cuckold, a man cast from her bed. Tricked too. I wanted nothing of Jane anymore and her backward ways. I watched, as though watching some ancient sport that was far away.

Then Jane picked up our heavy-bottomed iron frying pan, brandishing it like a club. *Nooooo!* Lilah let out a bloodcurdling yell, half screech, half snarl. She quaked, her eyes shot open. For the first time she was alarmed, screaming, pleading for mercy, up against the counter corner, covering her face with her arms.

Jane swung and struck Lilah hard – smack – on the shoulder and Lilah howled. Jane hit her quickly again, bashing Lilah's crumpled-over back, Lilah having sunk to the floor, shielding her head with her fists, dissolving, hissing. Pleading, "Please, please no more. I am dying. I am injured. No more. I will go, I will go. I am sorry." But Jane clubbed Lilah again and again, gathering her strength. Each time Lilah was more crippled. Was it something in Jane's choice of weapon? A substance Lilah couldn't touch?

"Stop," I shouted, but my voice was somehow mute. I was watching Lilah melt, before my eyes, the lover I'd waited for all my life. Her terror became mine, my blood boiled.

"Jane *stop,* you'll kill her," I intervened, grabbing Jane by the shoulders, prising her away; but Jane whirled round, jabbing me hard. I stumbled backwards, choking, my windpipe bruised. Jane was on Lilah again and this time I thought she might kill Lilah. Lilah crouched on the floor sobbing, "I am done for, it's all finished." Lilah was praying for her sins.

"Help me, help me."

"I am bleeding."

"You can have him, take him."

I took hold of Jane again, roughly, hauling her away bodily, kicking and screaming, and dragged her down the hallway. This time I was stirred: betrayal rose in me. I hated Jane. Nose to nose, face to face. Up against the wall. All Jane could do was weep. She blubbered she didn't mean it, she wanted to come back to me, she'd been stupid. But I knew she was simply too scared to have the courage of her convictions: her dreams and daydreams, her longings and innermost secrets. She would rather stay, cower with me, in our old life, in our chaste bed, than take off and find herself. She was free to go now. She should leave.

"Go," I said. "I want you to leave. Go. Find yourself. Isn't that what you want? I've heard you talking in your sleep. Take this opportunity, Jane. It's all over. Leave."

"I'm so sorry, Bill," Jane pleaded. My love for her had vanished. Dried up overnight. I wanted nothing more of our old charade. Lilah had shown me the man that had been lying rejected, the man in me who could no longer live like that. I wanted my cock sucked. I wanted my urges met. I wanted to be seen and celebrated as a man.

Lilah appeared in the hallway, her bruises were very evident. She was cold, a film blinked over her eyes. She sipped a glass of milk. Her hands were shaking.

*

Oh, Lilah was real. She was what Jane *hadn't* dreamt up – the firefly in the ointment. Lilah was a vibrant creature. Jane could never have simply imagined Lilah into being. Lilah's bruises rose up like stains, like ruptures, her blood clotting heavily, too clotted for her delicate skin, bulging underneath, as though she might haemorrhage if touched, if she happened to graze anything. A haemophiliac? I don't know. But the reaction to the iron was severe, a massive allergy. I was appalled, saying we should go to the nearest hospital. Lilah was deadly quiet, taking me by the hand and sitting me down on the sofa in our living room and saying that she would be helped by her own people. I thought she meant her family, that she needed to go back to America, that there was some kind of medication or vaccine, or even return to where she lived in London; maybe I could drive her home. But she put a finger to my lips. "Hush," she said. "You cannot help me now."

"What are you?"

In moments, in fragments, a hallucinatory feel came over me. Lilah's cream skin darkened to a deep moss brown, her ears elongated, her face raised up in lumps. Her eyes sealed up. She shivered and rocked back and forth. *Dear God!* Forgive me for my sins. I shook, clutching at my heart. I closed my eyes to banish the sight and when I opened them – Lilah was there again. A beautiful woman. Battered still, regarding me with exquisite candour. I loved her then and still. I loved our hours together. She showed me a thing or two. I would live differently from then on.

Soon after Jane left, Lilah left too, quietly, through the front door, wrapped up in one of my old coats. I watched her go, a small hunched figure, head bowed, eyes to the ground.

*

The house was wrecked. When both women had disappeared, it was then I became aware of the oppressive odour. Decaying meat? A rancid stink, something rotting.

"Choo Choo," I shouted, panicked. "Choo Choo," I bellowed, running outside, scanning the lawn, the tops of the fences. He knew his name and often responded, appearing like magic, one agile hop down from the fence post. Or, he'd cascade silently from a tree, landing tail up like a flag, sauntering towards me. It was around nine in the evening, still light. In the summer he stayed out for hours.

Indoors, chanting his name under my breath, images of Lilah's hideousness flashing before me. I guessed there had been a clash between them. I ran upstairs, looked into every room. The stench intensified as I ascended, a wretched God-awful dread flowed in my veins. What had Lilah done? The vile and wicked sprite, what had she done with Choo Choo? The smell was sharp, unmistakeable. The bathroom door was open. A wave of heat emanated from inside. The thermostat had been turned up. A sauna in there and the reek of death. The linen cupboard doors were flung open. Jane had been in, had taken her toiletries. The cabinet above the mirror was flung open and half-empty. My eyesight blurred, missing my wife already. I walked in, afraid to look into the cupboard.

There was Choo Choo, my beloved friend. The rage in his eyes was visceral, his body rigid. I wept like I never had before, like an infant, not through the breakup of my first marriage, not though my depression.

I found the fourth egg, soon afterwards, propped up on the windowsill in our bedroom, a nest of fuchsia tissue. My birthday wasn't far off; our wedding anniversary had just passed. Four years. It was a small egg, the smallest yet, but heavy in my hand, polished rock, caramel-red and when I looked closely, flecks of mauve and silver, opals.

When I searched later that day I couldn't find the other eggs Jane bought me; they had disappeared in the chaos of those twenty-four hours. Had Lilah stolen them? Did she destroy them like she destroyed Choo Choo? Or did Jane spirit them away with her when she left? I didn't know. They were gone. For days I carried the fourth egg with me everywhere I went, often clenched in my fist. I keep it next to me at night and gaze at it, all self-contained and benign, all feminine and pregnant with possibility. I thought about Jane a lot, wondered where she was. I had banished her. *Go*, I had said. I had given her full permission to leave. But in the aftermath of my tryst with Lilah I needed more. I wanted to ask Jane questions, as I always did. She was a beauty, my dear wife, enigmatic and thoughtful and always full of secrets. Are you happy now, Jane, my one true love – did you get what you desired?

7.
SEXY JANE

BILL

I was morose for days, a week? Maybe ten days passed. I couldn't work or eat. I didn't wash or change my clothes. I was alone in the house. No wife, Choo Choo dead. I buried him myself, in the garden with a spade, the same day both women vanished. I dug a hole under the oak tree in the back. I buried Choo Choo in the roots of the tree. I even said a prayer and how sorry I was and said 'goodbye my friend'. I decided I'd sell the house and move to the seaside or to France or Spain. I couldn't live in my mother's old house anymore; my childhood home. I would leave London for good. Or maybe I would just pack up and go travelling for a while, rent it out till it was sold. I would sell everything, auction the contents, give away what I could. Move far away, move on. I was verging on a major depression again. I missed Jane. I missed her presence and her voice. And Lilah? I felt used. Ridiculous. Middle-aged. I toyed with the idea of calling Sebastian, telling him everything. Why had she preyed on me and not him?

I didn't touch the tower Lilah had constructed. It stayed on my workbench for all that time. It didn't grow or change shape. But it continued to fascinate. I fancied it moved a little, as if it needed to breathe or to shift about now and then. It felt alive, somehow. I didn't even try to destroy it. In some strange way it was company – and it was *proof* of what had just happened. That Lilah had been here and ruined my life. I would stand in my workshop and stare at it for minutes at a time. What was it? I'd never been so alone before, so utterly bereft.

Over those days I also cleaned up the house. I mopped the kitchen floor and scrubbed away the purple stains with bleach, threw away the vegetables Lilah had used to pleasure herself. Days later, those scenes of carnality seemed unreal. I threw away the empty bottles of wine and champagne, the leftover cake. I washed the dishes and hoovered the living room and the hall. The small pile of fruit had rotted. I threw them away. In one day the house had been radically altered. We had let her in. We had invited this ruin. I began to restore our home again; but it didn't feel the same. It was as if the house had been violated. The fight between the two women echoed. I heard Jane's shrieks, Lilah's pain. I'd hated Jane then, and now there was no Jane. Our old life was eradicated. That was what she'd wanted; what I had wanted too. *Go away, Jane*, I'd said. I didn't know what to think, let alone say to anyone. I didn't answer calls.

*

It was early July. One morning I woke at dawn. I thought I heard something move downstairs and I was down there in an instant, searching for Lilah. Would she ever come back, could she, now she was so damaged? I stood alone, naked, in my home, and yet nothing around me felt familiar. Lilah hadn't returned. It started to rain. Something was missing; or rather, there was something *I* was missing. I felt like a man who'd been stolen from. Both women had disappeared and left behind them a sense of mystery. All life around me had been extinguished. Had I been cursed? Had Lilah left something of her spell behind? I'd cleaned the house, but nothing I had put back felt put right. I went back upstairs and pulled on some clothes. I remembered seeing Lilah insert the small stone inside her as she constructed the tower. What had she been doing? What else was inside that tower?

In my workshop I stared at her sculpture. It was beautiful. I liked it and also found it sinister. I decided to use my hands at first, pulling it apart piece by piece. I was surprised at how pliant and easy it came away in my hands, at how ingenious it was, a puzzle. It was textured and complicated. I took it apart, throwing the pieces that came away onto the floor. As I pulled and tugged the structure became more tightly knit. The first layer was effortless to dismantle; it more or less fell away in my hands. Pieces of old boot and crockery and bits of wood. It all came away. And then, inside, I saw she'd fitted together smaller objects. The crafty imp had stolen numerous trinkets from the baskets all around. Most of these things I had found, *objects trouvés*. They were someone else's once. Then they were mine. And then they were hers. Then – I stopped. Pieces of white creamy shell.

"No," I said aloud. No. Not that.

It was the ostrich egg Jane had given me years ago, a treasured gift. The egg was smashed all to pieces, and hidden there in the heart of the obelisk. I tugged quickly and more frantically at it, cursing under my breath. The pieces of white shell had been carefully and artfully inserted. I picked at the pieces and one by one pulled them out and laid them somewhere separate on the floor. I went back to the tower and pulled at it again to find the other eggs gifted to me by Jane. The egg made of turned beech wood, the small gaudy box; both had been hidden in the tower. Both I loved. Lilah had buried Jane's eggs deep inside. And then, it came to me, this was how she was punishing Jane; this was how she had managed to keep us apart. This was some kind of magic, made for me and Jane. Intuitively, I guessed. In amongst all *my* things Lilah had buried something precious of Jane's. Till then I'd only seen Lilah as a sex object, a star in my carnal fantasies. Only then I realised there was more of her, stupid oaf of a man that I was. She was a conniving predator; there was something of Lilah in my first wife too. She had also driven me mad with depression. Depression is a demon in itself. I had simply grasped towards Jane, hopeful for a better choice. Lilah had tampered with the order in our home, she had teased apart our life together.

I picked up a hammer from a line of hammers hanging in a row. I prised and smashed what was left of the tower apart. I found the small white and grey stone, her make-do 'jade egg', a sex toy she so happily jiggled inside herself. I fancied this must be an integral part of her hex. I remembered picking it up off a beach. I'd been with Jane. And I had watched, innocently, as Lilah had gone about her business of causing chaos with it. I put the small stone on the ground and smashed it so it splintered into many shards.

Lilah's sculpture was now demolished. Even so, I sensed it couldn't be that simple to destroy. I found a wheelbarrow and put all the pieces of the tower inside, including the eggs. I fancied this as some kind of vessel made of iron, the same element which could destroy Lilah.

I wheeled the vessel of loot outside. The ground was still damp from all the rain, and so I didn't try to build a fire. Instead I went back to my workshop, where I knew I kept some kerosene and emptied the can all over the contents of the barrow. I stood in the garden and thought of Jane. I was one half of our chaste dynamic. I'd *chosen* her for a wife. I'd selected cool Queen Jane and I had also been needy of her. I'd been a boy. I should have sold the house long ago, long before I even met Jane. Instead, I moved a woman into my mother's house. I'd idolised Jane and I'd given her this queenly status in my life. I hadn't seen this mistake. I had chosen Jane to replace my mother-queen.

I wanted a second chance. I wanted my wife Jane back. And so I lit a match and said an incantation to Aphrodite to reverse the spell cast on us by that wicked imp. "Out, Lilah," I shouted up into the cosmos. "Out wicked sprite." The flames hungrily fed on the contents of the barrow and I stood and watched for as long as it took, all the while mouthing the words, *come back to me, come back. The spell is broken. You are welcome home. You are invited back.*

That night I felt safer than I had in years. I realised I hadn't felt safe for some time. Secure of my future. I had been a man in recovery, waiting. I had only been half-alive. Choo Choo had been my protector. Jane had been my mother. I had assigned them the task of guardians. Now they were both gone and I was alone for the first time in my life – and I was scared and grateful at the same time. No more hiding. *I will live differently.* That night I slept soundly.

I dreamed of a snowball, presented as a gift to Jane. I dreamt that she had taken it away and watched it melt and drank the water. I dreamt of Jane's tender loins; I held a candle over them and dripped red wax onto her stomach and watched her hips writhe. I buried my tongue in the soft down between her legs and quenched a deep thirst. I heard her groan and drank some more. I saw a globe of Planet Earth inside a skip. I took it out and bounced it like a ball. I saw a mermaid hanging upside down from her tail, her mouth taped shut. I saw her try to scream for help. I saw Lilah too; I watched her wriggle around and dance, the beetroot ink drip from her mouth. She said, 'hello Mr Unfucked Bed, hello there you Half-Dead Son-of-a-Hag. I livened things up a bit, eh?' I saw Jane dancing naked across the kitchen. She wore a string of eggs around her neck. She stared at me and stroked herself and said 'I'm lonely here' and she began to stroke and touch herself.

I watched Jane on the countertop, her legs parted, her face placid. She slid her long fingers up and down and pleasured her soft wet cunt and said, "We haven't even spoken about the kissing yet." I woke hard as a post. I wondered about the fourth egg, I saw myself inserting it inside Jane and whispering words of love.

JANE

I found Bill still asleep in our bed. He was naked, covered to the waist by a thin sheet. It was dawn, a fragile time of the day. July too, and the sash window was fully open, the curtains not drawn. I hadn't seen Bill in ten days. Now, I feasted my eyes on him – so vulnerable in sleep. He was half-turned on his side, cradling himself with one arm, his hair had grown decidedly longer and fell about his face and shoulders, and his torso was summer tanned. He was a man in his late 40s and big framed, both muscular and voluptuous, a sight of a man. Gazing down at him there, I came to understand that Bill was a piece of my puzzle too. Just like Lilah, he was part of my solution. A longing for him sprang inside me, warm and reassuring – my husband. I put a hand across my belly and welcomed the sensation, letting it spread slowly, thinking I had needed Bill all along, for part of me to heal.

And now I saw him lying there, I had a choice. I could go, leave him sleeping. Or I could step forward into another life, fully open. On the side table next to him, I saw the small polished egg I'd left behind, a part of me too. A gift, a message I'd never fully understood myself. I took out the stick of chalk I had with me and bent to the ground, drawing a thin white line around our bed, whispering incantations. The sprite had gone but she had left her energy in the room; I could still smell her there, dense earth. I lit a small sprig of sage too and uttered banishments at each corner of the room and when I was done, I sat down carefully on the bed. I had never fought for Bill, let alone protected him or what we had.

Bill's eyes flickered.

I smiled at him. He groaned and shook his head. His eyes flew open and he stared. His alarm faded when he registered who it was.

"I'm here," I said.

His eyes opened wider, his long hair fell over his face and he pulled it back. His beard looked stronger too, as though Bill had been quietly growing richer over the last week or so. He didn't say anything; he just looked at me. He gazed and mouthed the words *hello, Jane*.

He looked clear-faced and older. The worriedness I'd associated with his features had somehow lifted. I said hello back and moved across the bed and lay myself down next to him, face to face, our bodies aligned and close, not touching. I was clothed. Bill was naked. The sheet separated us. We gazed at each other for several minutes. Sadness swelled in me, a wave of regret and devastation at the loss of him. For those ten days I'd been unable to contact him by phone or email. Lilah had interfered. I had understood some kind of separation had been imposed; it was out of my control. We'd been cursed. I'd wept for days in a hotel room. Tears fell, looking at him. He touched my cheek.

"I'm sorry," I said.

He moved closer and kissed my tears. I felt relaxed, like that tender feeling after a bath. Or maybe my own grief had softened me. I felt older too, and womanly, and forgiving of myself and him. Bill kissed me on the mouth and pulled away the sheet and I reached down to hold him.

I kissed him back and he moved across me, pulling open the buttons of my shirt. Then we were together, in motion, kissing, responsive to each other, tongues searching, words flowing between us. My back arched as he smothered my breasts with kisses and whispers of his own sadness and regret. Both of us uttered our mantras, *sorry, sorry* for the past. I was wet and soft and half-clothed.

I saw Bill then. Big-boned and full-hipped and sexy. Both of us were somehow sexier for being this age. Had I lost confidence in my body? If so, I seemed to suddenly have it back. Then Bill was on top of me, naked and hard, his cock pressed into my stomach. He peeled off my white lace bra and I showed him that I was a little unsure of my breasts and he said 'yes' with his eyes. Had this been part of it? The loss of my younger body, was that also in the mix? Bill peeled down my jeans, taking my panties with them. He sank his mouth between my legs and I gasped, burying one hand in his hair. I laughed and he laughed too and drank. I opened my legs and sighed and opened my eyes and even said the word out loud, "Lilah".

I could feel her presence in the glossy silkiness between my legs. Bill's tongue was strong and agile and I writhed with the pleasure he provoked. Then he stopped and looked at me, as if to say, *this is only beginning*. He pulled my jeans away so that I was naked and yes, my nakedness brought on a feeling of extreme shyness. And at the same time I felt open and full of longing. Then Bill was using his knuckle up and down, up and down on my clitoris, stroking me and dripping his silky serum on to me. My breath quickened and a spasm came from my groin, from his tender loving hands. An orgasm sprang upwards from my centre and swept through me. I'd never known this husband-lover Bill, had never tempted him to me, ever. He laughed and watched my body tremble and then he said "my wife, my wife", and slowly, oh so slowly, he sank his long hard cock into me.

*

Weeks later, we were in Madrid. A small apartment lent to us by a friend. It had a tiny balcony which looked down onto a square in the centre of the city. The summer nights were hot and humid and the square filled every night with young people drinking gallons of cheap red wine mixed with *Coca Cola*, a local elixir. We would watch young couples dragging each other down alleyways to copulate and we would climb over the balcony onto the rooftop where there was a slanted slate roof.

In the heat of those Spanish summer nights we made love on the rooftop of our apartment block, hot and hard and rough sometimes, like dogs, or like the young people in the square. Sometimes Bill would fuck me from behind, me bent over the balcony rail, watching the young people fuck, getting off on the sight of their fucking. We fucked while watching them fuck – and it was glorious and even dangerous to be spotted up there. My centre was always soft and swollen and *al fresco* fucking became something of a new delight. And of course, I discovered a love of that ancient art once only practiced by whores – fellatio.

One evening we were up there on the rooftop holding hands, laying on our backs, half-clothed. Those were the first days of a new era. We had so much to explore, a pure and simple happiness had come to us from our new experience of sexually loving each other. Eros, could also be pure! This was what neither of us had expected. We lay on the roof together and Bill moved a little so he could rest his head in my lap. Nothing about our old life existed anymore. The house was up for sale. It was late August, the summer drawing to a close. We'd decided to go travelling for the foreseeable future, fuck our way across the cities of Europe and its many rooftops. I gazed down at Bill's head in my lap and realised that my hunch about Lilah had been right after all. I'd invited her in – and she'd given us a fright. And I mourned her loss from the world of men, and yet I had somehow known Lilah all along. A part of her was me, and I was partly Lilah now.

AUTHOR'S NOTE

I've been working on this book, on and off, for fourteen years. It has grown slowly and been through many drafts, following me from home to home and onto three different computers. When I began *The Tryst*, in 2002, people didn't own iPhones, you could smoke in a British pub and *The Independent* was still in print. So, this book has taken so long it's dated over the years of writing it. Knowing the perils and the shame that writing about the subject of sex attracts, I also wondered if I should use a pseudonym; so, at different points I experimented with a *nom de plume*, one or two of which were outright ridiculous. There were all sorts of ideas and false starts and of course I wrote and published other books in those years. But I always came back to this small, sexy novel, though, because I had faith in it. In the last five years, it has been sold twice. This novel had a will of its own; it demanded to be published.

So, a very warm thanks to my dear old friends Sean Thomas and Clare Martin for reading the early drafts; also thanks to Kian de la Cour for a subsequent read closer to completion. Thanks to my agent Isobel Dixon for staying the course and much good advice, and for Sam Mills, my editor, at Dodo Ink, for making this a better book and for being the daring editor this book deserves. And thanks, also, to all the tantrikas, kinksters, sex workers, teachers and practitioners, conscious lovers and friends I've met on the path in the last ten years.

You all inspired a transition, a crossing over, into another world of loving and sexing. I knew it was there, waiting for me. Thank you.

At Dodo Ink, we're book lovers first and foremost. From finding a great manuscript to the moment it hits the bookshop shelves, that's how we approach the publishing process at every stage: excited about giving you something we hope you'll love. Good books aren't extinct, and we want to seek out the best literary fiction to bring to you. A great story shouldn't be kept from readers because it's considered difficult to sell or can't be put in a category. When a reader falls in love with something, they tell another reader, and that reader tells another. We think that's the best way of selling a book there is.

Dodo Ink was founded by book lovers, because we believe that it's time for publishing to pull itself back from the brink of extinction and get back to basics: by finding the best literary fiction for people who love to read. Books shouldn't be thought of in terms of sales figures, and neither should you. We approach every step of the process thinking of how we would want a book to be, as a reader, and give it the attention it deserves. When you see our Dodo logo, we'd like you to think of our books as recommendations from one book lover to another. After all, aren't those the ones that we take the greatest pleasure in?

At Dodo Ink, we know that true book lovers are interested in stories regardless of genre or categorisation. That's how we think a publishing company should work, too: by giving the reader what they want to read, not what the industry thinks they should. We look for literary fiction that excites, challenges, and makes us want to share it with the world. From finding a manuscript to designing the cover, Dodo Ink books reflect our passion for reading. We hope that when you pick up one of our titles, you get the same thrill—that's the best thank you we can think of.

www.dodoink.com